THE MAN WHO LED A DREAM LIFE

THE MAN WHO LED A DREAM LIFE

A STEWART HOAG MYSTERY

DAVID HANDLER

THE MYSTERIOUS PRESS
NEW YORK

THE MAN WHO LED A DREAM LIFE

Mysterious Press
An Imprint of Penzler Publishers
58 Warren Street
New York, N.Y. 10007

First Mysterious Press edition

Interior design by Lia Kantrowitz

Library of Congress Control Number: 2025942792

ISBN: 978-1-61316-732-8
eBook ISBN: 978-1-61316-733-5

10 9 8 7 6 5 4 3 2 1

Printed in the United States of America
Distributed by Simon & Schuster

For Elaine Pagliaro, who has been doing her best to keep me honest for decades. Thank you, my wise friend.

THE MAN WHO LED A DREAM LIFE

CHAPTER ONE

In case you've ever wondered, Merilee and I officially tied the knot at city hall on the cold, blustery morning of January 11, 1983, which was three months after we'd first set eyes on each other in the Blue Mill on Commerce Street in Greenwich Village. As I sit here now, twelve years later, it still ranks as the happiest moment of my life. We'd decided to tell no one we were getting hitched because we both led such public lives. Merilee was the gorgeous, six-foot-tall blond star of stage and screen who'd already won an Oscar and a Tony by the age of twenty-eight. I was the novelist who the *New York Times* Book Review had labeled "the first major new literary voice of the 1980s." *Time* magazine had even plastered my picture on its cover under a headline that read: THE VOICE OF A NEW GENERATION? We considered our wedding to be a private occasion. Ours.

Merilee wore a white Armani dress. I wore my navy blue suit from Strickland and Sons, Savile Row, with a sparkling white shirt and pink-and-blue bow tie. If she was nervous, Merilee didn't show it one bit. I was plenty calm myself. The fact that I'd nicked my right earlobe with Grandfather's straight razor that morning and it had bled for a solid half hour was strictly coincidental.

My college chum, Ezra Spooner, who'd been with me that night at the Blue Mill and introduced me to the woman who would become the great love of my life, stood up for me. Merilee's favorite cousin, Phoebe, a willowy blond beauty who seemed to be in an oddly somber mood, stood up for her. And our basset hound puppy, Lulu, formerly known as Princess Flavia, stood up for both of us, sporting a royal blue ascot. She was almost four months old when we'd adopted her, and she was a finicky eater who'd weighed only eighteen pounds and was all ears, nose, and paws. She was now nearly seven months old and was finally starting to grow into her ears. Okay, I just lied to you about her ears. But she did weigh thirty-two pounds thanks to our discovery that she loved 9Lives mackerel . . . for cats. She had unusual eating habits. Her favorite snacks were anchovies. Not exactly a normal dog, but we were not exactly normal people.

The city clerk, a crisp, efficient Latino in his fifties, didn't mind Lulu being there for the occasion. I imagine he'd seen his share of odd witnesses. I doubt a pet seal would have thrown him.

After we'd slipped gold wedding rings onto the third finger of each other's left hand and he'd rattled off a bunch of words I don't remember, he officially pronounced Stewart Stafford Hoag and Merilee Gilbert Nash man and wife.

By then tears were streaming down Merilee's beautiful face. When I kissed her and held her in my arms, she blubbered, "I'm so happy."

"That goes double for me, Blondie."

Ez gave her a kiss on the cheek, grinning. Phoebe kissed me softly on the lips, her own eyes filled with tears.

And just like that, we were married.

We'd picked the perfect day, it turned out, because on that very same day, the Yankees' blowhard owner, George Steinbrenner, was holding a major press event up in the Bronx to announce he was hiring combative, seldom sober Billy Martin to be his manager for the third time. So there were no freelance tabloid photographers waiting outside to mob us when we emerged into the winter chill.

It would, we hoped, take a day before word of our nuptials leaked out, and by then we'd be honeymooning for a week in the Enchanted Cottage, the snowy retreat outside of Brattleboro, Vermont, that belonged to Merilee's aunt Betsy. It had always been Merilee's favorite place, and it had been her girlhood dream to honeymoon there. Since our red 1958 Jaguar XK150 was not exactly designed for the snow, I'd rented a 1982 Land Rover from Rocco, who owned the garage where we stored the Jag. We intended to go for romps in the snow with Lulu, drink twenty-one-year-old Balvenie single malt Scotch in front of the huge stone fireplace, and burrow in wedded bliss under a heap of Hudson Bay blankets.

Right now, the occasion called for a bottle of Dom Pérignon at her parents' Charlton Street town house. It was the house Merilee had grown up in. We'd been staying in it while they were away for several months in Argentina. Merilee's dad imported minerals or something. Ez had to get back to the office, but Phoebe, who was wearing a beautiful black cashmere pantsuit, joined us as we caught a cab home. Since it was chilly in the old town house, I chopped some kindling in the basement with a hatchet and built us a roaring fire in the living room fireplace out of well-seasoned applewood logs.

Happily, I'd almost completely recovered from the serious left trapezius wound I'd suffered in the fall. I was still working with a physical therapist three times a week and, on the off days, swimming for forty-five minutes in the pool at the Racquet and Tennis Club. I was also squeezing a tennis ball one hundred times every morning to regain the strength in my left hand, although it was hard to find one that Lulu hadn't converted into a saliva-soaked chew toy. But I was able to type again on my beloved 1958 solid steel Olympia manual portable. Had even sent a new short story to my agent, Alberta Pryce, aka the Silver Fox, which the *New Yorker* had purchased. Alberta was pleased that I was back at the typewriter again, but when she asked me if I'd come up with an idea for a second novel yet, I had to confess that I hadn't.

Merilee had spent the past two weeks doing table readings of David Mamet's latest work in progress. He had cast her for the lead role opposite Al Pacino and Mary Beth Hurt. She was thrilled beyond belief. Meanwhile, Robert Altman kept calling her from the Coast about a film he wanted her to star in, although she had no idea what it was because he had nothing down on paper yet.

I chilled three glasses, popped the cork on a bottle of 1966 Dom Pérignon, and we drank to our special day. Phoebe sat there on the sofa in what continued to be an oddly somber mood.

She was twenty-seven, a year younger than Merilee, and had long golden hair very much like her famous cousin, but her eyes were a pale blue in contrast to Merilee's luminous green. And while she was tall and leggy, she was more delicately constructed, with narrow shoulders. She was a gentle, sensitive woman. Her favorite activities were reading poetry and playing the violin in an amateur chamber music group. She had attended the high-toned private Brearley School same as Merilee did—until, that is, Merilee's parents shipped her off to Miss Porter's School in Farmington, Connecticut, which her mother had attended. After graduating from

Wellesley, Phoebe had returned to Brearley as an English teacher.

Not that she needed to work to put food on the table. She was married to the charismatic, globetrotting adventurer Junior Singleton, who'd been the most prized catch in New York when the demure Phoebe snagged him. The scion of one of New York City's elite four hundred families of wealthy social aristocrats that dated back to the Gilded Age, Junior was reputedly worth $200 million. His parents had been killed in a car crash in Mexico when he was a teenager. Since he was an only child, the entire fortune and the freedom that went with it had fallen his way.

Phoebe and Junior did not, by temperament, seem to be an obvious match. But once Junior made it clear that he was smitten by her graceful beauty, Phoebe's dragon lady of a mother, Pippa Trowbridge, the all-powerful editor in chief of *SHE*, America's top women's fashion magazine, went to work on Phoebe to win him over. Phoebe was thoroughly intimidated by her overbearing mother and obeyed Pippa's every wish. The same could not be said of Phoebe's father, Howard, a real estate developer who'd divorced Pippa four years ago and married one of her magazine's cover models—who happened to be a year younger than Phoebe. The two of them were living happily ever after three thousand miles away in Santa Barbara.

I've learned that there's no such thing as a "typical" marriage, but Phoebe and Junior's was hardly what most people would classify as a marriage at all. Just for starters, they were seldom on the same continent together. He'd successfully climbed to the summit of Mount Everest twice, competed in the European Grand Prix circuit in a Formula 1 Ferrari, was an expert downhill racer who took on the most challenging slopes in the Swiss Alps, surfed twenty-foot curls in Maui, and flew hang gliders in Kahului. His investment manager, a Brit, had access to an office in New York, but Junior preferred to meet with him in London and unwind in the Devon countryside while Phoebe stayed home in New York teaching school. It was her job. Junior had no job—didn't need one. He simply pursued what most men would consider a dream life, which included sleeping with any woman who struck his fancy. The man was a major philanderer.

After I topped off our glasses and fed the fire, I sat back down in one of the easy chairs. Lulu climbed into my lap and made herself comfortable, which is one of her specialties.

"I've always been fond of this old house," Phoebe said, gazing around.

Merilee sighed. "Me, too. But my folks will be coming back in March, so we have to start looking for a place of our own. Hoagy has his heart set on a prewar high-rise on Central Park West."

"With a minimum of eight windows overlooking the park," I reminded her.

"Is that written in stone?" Phoebe sounded disappointed.

Merilee shot a curious glance at me before she said, "Why do you ask?"

"Our town house will be going on the market next week. We're selling it. Or I should say I'm selling it. It's officially mine now. Has been for two whole weeks. I've divorced Junior, you see," she said quietly, running a long, slender index finger around the rim of her glass.

Merilee gaped at her in shock. "When did all of this happen?"

"I filed four months ago. We weren't meant to be together. We weren't together. I never saw him. Junior didn't contest it, because all I asked for was one million dollars and our town house on East Sixty-Eighth Street, which I intend to sell. It's much too big for one person. Mother went totally berserk. She wanted me to hold out for half of Junior's fortune. But I don't want it. Besides, my Realtor, Siena Bing, who is absolutely the top Realtor in the East Sixties, thinks I'll clear more than three million on the house because it's so beautiful. I'll be able to buy a comfy two-bedroom co-op and still have plenty left over for a cozy country place in the Berkshires, where I can garden and enjoy some peace and quiet. My old Brearley classmate, Bob Ackerman, is a lawyer with a good firm. He not only handled it for me but put me in touch with a financial planner who's investing my cash settlement in safe mutual funds and tax-free municipal bonds. I'll be set for life."

Merilee was still in a state of shock. "You filed for the divorce four months ago? Why haven't you said one word to me about it?"

"Because it was too upsetting to talk about. Junior slept with other women by the dozen. I just couldn't stand it any longer. I honestly don't know why he married me. We had zero in common. I should have turned him down. But he's such an expert flatterer that he convinced me he loved me and me alone.

And Mother was so determined I marry him that I said yes."

I knew Junior reasonably well. We were at Harvard together and shared social connections through the Racquet and Tennis Club and the super-exclusive, highly secretive Lunch Club, which was a group of handpicked artists, adventurers, visionary politicians, and academics who met once a week to exchange stimulating conversation and gourmet meals around a big table in a town house in Murray Hill. I'd been invited to join when I was crowned as a major new literary voice and was so curious to find out who else belonged that I couldn't resist the opportunity. It turned out that Junior had been a member for several years due to his Everest exploits. Just last week, I'd been seated next to the charismatic former New York mayor John Lindsay and was pleased to learn that he'd admired my novel.

Across the table, Junior had been chatting not so amiably with Dr. Jill Perlo, the MIT climatologist who'd recently published a controversial study in *Scientific American* warning that if the planet continued to get warmer at its present rate and the US population continued to mushroom, the entire American Southwest would run out of water by the year 2030. Dr. Perlo, a lean, sinewy blonde in her thirties who was an expert rock climber, had seemed furious with Junior. In fact, after telling him off in a low, threatening voice, she'd thrown down her napkin and stormed out before our choucroute arrived.

Another of his romantic entanglements gone awry, I'd assumed.

"I swear to you," Phoebe said, "that I'll never let Mother bully me again. She bullies everyone. She drove Father away. She drives away every promising young editor who works for her. And God knows she's bullied me ever since I was a little girl. I was so afraid of her I used to have a stammer, remember, Merilee?"

Merilee blinked at her. "I'd forgotten."

"I had to take speech therapy to get rid of it."

"So are you living in the house all by yourself now?" I asked her.

"No, I've been staying with Meredith, a teacher friend from Brearley who has an extra bedroom, while Siena gets the house 'fluffed,' as she calls it. She has a handyman touching up the paint and grout, a bit of dry rot in an upstairs windowsill, that sort of thing. Once she puts it on the market, she's positive she can move it within a week."

"It is beautiful." Merilee glanced at me. "You've never seen it, have you, darling?"

"I have not."

Phoebe lowered her eyes, coloring slightly. "It seems so inappropriate to be having this conversation when we're supposed to be celebrating your wedding, but as it happens, there's more. I'm romantically involved with the cellist in my chamber music group, Barry Zallinger. He's a Park Avenue ophthalmologist who couldn't be more Junior's opposite. He's studious, serious, and devoted to his patients. Not exactly handsome but appealing. And he adores me. Couldn't believe I was willing to go out to dinner with him. He keeps calling himself the luckiest man in the world, as if I'm someone special."

I topped off their champagne glasses before I refilled my own, emptying the bottle. "You are someone special, Phoebe. Hell, if it weren't for Merilee, I'd marry you."

Merilee snorted. "You're an hour too late, writer boy."

"Barry's also gentle and giving, unlike Junior, who treats sex like it's strictly for his own gratification. Junior's over and done with before the sheets are even warm. Barry's happy to just hold me in his arms for hours. He loves me."

"Has your mother met him yet?" Merilee asked.

"No, and I'm determined that she never will. She'll disapprove of him and drive him away. Meanwhile, there's the town house to dispose of. I'm anxious to move it quickly and be done with it. But if you two . . ." Lulu let out a small yip of protest. "Excuse me, you three are at all interested, I'd accept a lower price. Call it a family discount. The only thing is you'll have to decide fast."

"But Hoagy has his heart set on a Central Park West high-rise with a view of the park, remember?" Merilee pointed out.

I said, "We're also leaving for our honeymoon in Vermont this afternoon. We'll be gone for a week."

"Of course." Phoebe seemed crestfallen. She really wanted us to buy it. Or so it seemed.

"But that doesn't mean we couldn't take a run over there right now and take a quick look at it." I was curious to see it, I must admit.

Phoebe brightened. "You'll love the paneled library on the second floor. You'd be so at home writing there. It has five bedrooms, five and a half baths, a live-in maid's room, a laundry room, and central air-conditioning. There's even a garden for Lulu to romp around in."

"It really is a lovely house, darling," Merilee said brightly.

"So let's go take a look. We'll still be able to make it up to the Enchanted Cottage by suppertime."

"Let's," Merilee agreed.

And so off we went.

If only I'd kept my big mouth shut.

If only.

CHAPTER TWO

The town house that now belonged to Phoebe and Phoebe alone was situated smack dab in a neighborhood of single-family town houses on East Sixty-Eighth Street between Park and Madison that was so choice it was commonly known as Millionaire's Row. Hers was an immaculate four-story red-brick neo-Georgian that had been built in 1887, she informed us as we sped uptown in the back seat of a Checker cab. The cabbie was listening to Michael Jackson's "Thriller" on the radio, a song that was inescapable that season.

I paid the cabbie after he'd pulled up at the wrought iron gate out front and then put Lulu on her leash and got out as Phoebe unlocked the gate. After she'd unlocked the dead bolt lock in the paneled hardwood front door and swung it open, we heard women's voices inside. They were coming from the kitchen, an immense gourmet kitchen that featured a six-burner Aga stove, a double-door refrigerator, and a separate double-door freezer. The kitchen also served as the dining room, with a farmhouse-style trestle table that could seat twelve.

One of the voices, an authoritative bellow that could be heard across the river in Elmhurst, Queens, belonged to Phoebe's fifty-something mother, Pippa Trowbridge, whom I'd met a couple of times. The other belonged to a petite, shapely woman in her late thirties with stylishly layered auburn hair who was decked out in a Ralph Lauren navy blue blazer and tailored slacks. She had a golden tan that came from either a week in St. Bart's or a bottle of bronzer. It gave her a healthy glow, although it did not manage to hide the dark circles under her eyes.

"Oh, hi, Phoebe!" she said brightly, stifling a phlegmy cough. "I was hoping you'd stop by. I'm just checking up on my interior decorator's finishing touches. I think it looks fabulous. I hope you do, too."

Phoebe said, "Siena, say hello to my cousin, Merilee, and Stewart Hoag."

"It's an honor to meet you both. I'm a huge fan, Merilee, and Stewart—"

"Make it Hoagy."

"Hoagy, I loved your book so much I gave copies of it to everyone in my office. I won't shake hands because I meet so many prospective buyers every day that I seem to catch every cold and flu bug that's making the rounds."

"Nice to meet you," I said. "The short stack is Lulu."

"Well, hi, sweetie!"

Lulu let out a yip, moseyed over, and got her ears scrunched.

"Bassets don't shed, am I right?" Siena asked cautiously.

"That's correct."

"Good, because I'm trying to keep the place as spotless as possible," she said, stifling another cough.

Pippa, who was nearly as tall and slender as Phoebe, carried herself with a tremendous air of elegance and authority. She was dressed in Gucci from head to toe, wore her hair cropped at her chin and so expertly dyed frosted blond that it was impossible to tell how gray it was or wasn't. She had intense blue eyes that were set in a permanent glare and never blinked, which took some getting used to, as did her brand-new face, which was so utterly free of lines, wrinkles, and furrows that it resembled a live-action airbrushed photo. She looked no older than Siena as she stood there jangling a set of house keys in her manicured hand. Evidently, she had a set of her own to the place, although she lived in a doorman building on East Seventy-Second Street. But it was common practice in New York City for women to keep a spare set of keys with a friend or relative who lived nearby so they wouldn't get locked out if their purse got snatched.

"Merilee, why on earth did you bring that ridiculous puppy here?" she demanded of her famous niece.

Lulu immediately retreated between my legs, whimpering. She's very sensitive to insults.

"Because we're here to look at the house and she's a member of the family," Merilee replied serenely.

"Well, I think she's adorable," said Siena, who was no slouch at sucking up to prospective clients.

Phoebe said, "Merilee and Hoagy are leaving town this afternoon for a week, and I wanted them to have a sneak peek because I'm not sure it'll still be on the market by the time they get back."

"Wouldn't surprise me one bit," Siena agreed. "It's a gem."

"And I stopped by," Pippa said coldly to Phoebe, "because when I called you at Brearley this morning, you weren't in yet and didn't return my call. I tried the apartment where you've been staying with your coworker, but all I got was her answering machine. I was hoping I might find you here. I've had another conversation with my lawyer. He's convinced that you're letting a hundred million dollars slip through your fingers and don't seem to realize it."

Phoebe let out a pained sigh. "Mother, we've discussed my divorce settlement twenty times. There's nothing more to talk about. It's my marriage, my house, my life, and I'll live it as I choose. Why can't you respect that?"

"Well, you needn't be huffy with me."

"I'm not being huffy, although I would appreciate it if you'd go back to the office and leave us alone. You're spoiling what has been a very festive day."

"What's so festive about it?" she demanded.

"Merilee and Hoagy got married this morning."

Siena said, "Congratulations! You know what, Hoagy? I can think of an awfully wonderful wedding present."

I smiled at her. "How did I know you were going to say that?"

"Married?" Pippa roared in outrage. "What do you mean they got married? Why didn't I hear about this? Why wasn't I invited?"

"No one was," I said. "We wanted it to be a private civil ceremony at city hall. Didn't tell a soul."

Now Pippa was practically licking her chops. "Do you mean that you two are married and no one in New York knows about it yet?"

"Correct. And we'd appreciate it if it stayed that way," I said, knowing perfectly well she would blab it to Liz Smith and Cindy Adams within the hour and no one would be talking about anything else that evening at Elaine's, the popular glitterati restaurant/watering hole. But we'd be in Vermont by then and needn't return any of the phone calls on our answering machines.

"Do you mind if I show them around myself?" Phoebe asked Siena.

"Of course not. It's your house. But I'll stick around in case they decide to make us an offer in the next thirty minutes."

"I will, too," Pippa said defiantly.

Phoebe rolled her eyes. "Do whatever you want, Mother. It's not as if I've ever been able to stop you."

"I am not impressed by your attitude, young lady," Pippa fumed.

Phoebe let out a cascade of laughter. "That was perfect, Mother. So totally you." Then she smiled at us and said, "Let's start the grand tour, shall we?" She steered us across the parquet-floored entry hall, where a curved stairway led up to the second floor. "That door under the stairs is the powder room. And the hallway next to the kitchen leads to the maid's room and laundry room."

"Do you have a live-in maid?" I asked.

"No, just a cleaning lady, Katie Healey, who comes in three days a week from Rockaway. Her daughter, Bridget, has started helping her out lately because Katie has a bad hip and lugging a vacuum up three flights of stairs is no fun."

We followed Phoebe into a high-ceilinged living room with a woodburning fireplace and French doors that led out to a patio and the garden. Matching leather sofas faced each other across a coffee table that consisted of two antique steamer trunks laid end to end and topped with a slab of glass. The trunks were plastered with the labels of transatlantic shipping lines and luxurious European hotels from a bygone era. They were very interesting to look at. The paintings on the wall weren't. They were just blobs of color. But the immense, gently aged Afghan area rug was quite beautiful.

Lulu pawed at the French door, whimpering. She wanted to check out the garden.

"You'd better stay inside, little pard," I said. "Siena will get mad if your muddy paws mess up the floors. My apologies, but there's an anchovy in it for you when we get home."

Lulu snuffled, mollified, and we returned to the stairway.

Siena and Pippa were still in the kitchen. Siena was busy jabbering away on the phone. Pippa was busy glaring at Phoebe. She was so peeved that she practically had steam coming out of her nostrils like an angry hippo in a Disney cartoon. Phoebe excused herself and ducked into the powder room.

"What's up with Pippa's face?" I whispered to Merilee. "Did somebody take a sandblaster to it?"

"I'll bet she's seeing Dr. Lookgood," she whispered in response.

"Who's he?"

"You're familiar with Dr. Feelgood, the one who shoots up the Truman Capote set with all sorts of illegal drugs? Well, Dr. Lookgood is a high-society cosmetic surgeon who dabbles in expensive injections that aren't FDA approved."

"Such as . . . ?"

"Botox, which relaxes the muscles in your face, and collagen, which makes your lips look as if you've been stung by a nest of wasps. I know a couple of aging actresses who are doing it, and it's not wise. They may look younger, but performers need full command of their facial muscles and lips to register emotions. You'd never catch me doing that."

Phoebe rejoined us, and we started our way up to the second floor. With her short legs, Lulu had trouble with the Charlton house's steep wooden stairs. These were shallower, and carpeted, and she had a much easier time with them.

The second-floor front room was every writer's fantasy office—paneled in cherry with floor-to-ceiling bookshelves and a circa-1920 walnut desk worthy of a bank president. Tall windows overlooked the street.

There was a private bath and a kitchenette with a mini fridge and coffee maker.

"I'll miss this room," Phoebe confessed. "I used to set up my music stand in here and practice whenever Junior was off on one of his adventures."

"Nice globe," I said, admiring the antique globe on a table in the corner. I went over to it, peering at the United States closely. "Oklahoma was still a territory when it was made." Oklahoma was granted statehood in 1907. "I'm surprised Junior left this beauty behind."

"It's not his. Siena borrowed it from her interior decorator, same as that modern art in the living room."

"I didn't think those paintings seemed like your taste," Merilee said.

"They're not. I have a small collection of early twentieth-century line drawings and etchings that I'm currently storing in Mother's apartment until I get a place of my own. And Junior took whatever was precious to him when the divorce was settled."

"Did Siena's decorator supply the living room furniture and this desk, too?" I asked.

"No, the furniture's mine, but Siena thinks the house shows better with it here. After it sells, I'll put the furniture in storage until she finds me the apartment I want."

"Where is Junior living these days?"

"He's taken a suite at the Sherry-Netherland," she said coolly. "But I made sure he held on to a set of keys in case he remembered something he wanted."

"That was nice of you," Merilee said.

"I do want to be civil about this whole thing. It's not as if he's a thief. Besides, when the house sells, they'll change all of the locks."

We moved on. There was a vast expanse of linen closets lining the second-floor hallway toward the back of the house, where a spacious guest bedroom and bath overlooked the patio and garden.

"What a lovely view," Merilee murmured appreciatively.

"Up the stairs we go," Phoebe said as we continued climbing. "The entire third floor is the master suite. There are two more bedrooms and baths on the fourth floor, which, in Siena-speak, makes it the 'consummate' family home."

The master suite was nothing to sneer at. There was a king-sized bed. A seating area with leather armchairs and a twenty-seven-inch Sony television. A workout space equipped with a rowing machine and an Exercycle. The master bath had twin sinks, a stall shower, a bathtub, and a sauna.

"I've always coveted your sauna," Merilee said. "So good for the pores."

"There's no need to covet it any longer," Phoebe responded teasingly. "Just buy the place."

There were walk-in his and hers dressing rooms. The door to hers was open. Its contents were mostly cleared out aside from some summer clothes. The door to Junior's dressing room was shut. As we started toward it, Lulu let out a whimper and backed away.

I frowned at her. "What is it, girl?"

"Maybe she hears a mouse in there. She's terrified of them," Merilee explained to Phoebe.

"I doubt that," Phoebe responded. "Siena made sure the house was exterminated two weeks ago. There's nothing she doesn't think of."

As Phoebe approached the door and started to open it, Lulu let out a low moan and backed farther away—all the way out to the hallway.

Merilee frowned at her. "What's wrong, sweetness?"

When Phoebe opened it, we found out what was wrong—Junior Singleton was curled up on the floor in there wearing a wool fisherman's sweater and corduroy trousers, and smelling none too fresh due to the Claude Dozorme polished rosewood steak knife that someone had plunged deep into his left eyeball. Lulu, being a world-class scent hound, had been able to pick up the smell of death through the closed door. We hadn't. The three of us stood there, frozen, gazing at Junior in silent horror.

Right up until Phoebe let out an ear-piercing scream.

CHAPTER THREE

After I phoned it in, we sat in the living room with Phoebe and Pippa, stunned and shaken. Siena gave us our privacy by remaining at the kitchen table, although she seemed quite upset herself at this ghastly turn of events at her prime East Side listing. She was now sniffling and dabbing at her eyes with a tissue in addition to coughing.

Two patrol cars arrived in no time. Four patrolmen tromped upstairs to have a look at Junior Singleton for themselves, speaking to each other in low, respectful tones.

"I should call Rocco and cancel that Land Rover," I said to Merilee. "We'll go to the Enchanted Cottage next week."

Merilee nodded grimly. "Absolutely."

"But you mustn't," Phoebe protested. "This is your wedding day."

"That doesn't matter now," Merilee said. "We're family and we're not leaving you. You'll stay with us tonight in our guest room. I have clothes you can wear and cosmetics galore in the master bath."

"Nonsense," Pippa huffed. "You'll stay with me. You should be with your mother at a time like this."

"Oh, don't be absurd," Phoebe said to her angrily.

I gathered that gentle, mild-mannered Phoebe didn't usually speak to her overbearing mother that way. Briefly, Pippa sat there with her mouth open and no words coming out. Then, red-faced, she got up and stormed into the kitchen to join Siena. Within seconds, I could hear her making a phone call.

"Are you sure about this?" Phoebe asked Merilee, ignoring her mother's outrage. "This is your wedding night, after all."

"Positive. You're staying with us," Merilee said as Lulu climbed up into Phoebe's lap and rested her head on her shoulder.

"Thank you, Lulu," Phoebe said, stroking her. "You're a sweetie."

"Lulu is the official Charlton house comfort mechanism," I said.

Phoebe let out a mournful sigh. "This is totally my fault, you know."

Merilee studied her curiously. "What's totally your fault?"

"If I hadn't filed for a divorce, Junior would still be alive."

"I have to disagree," Merilee said. "Your marriage was over and done with ages ago. You told us so. Besides, we have no idea who killed him or why. That's up to the police to figure out. So don't beat up on yourself."

"They'll want us out of here pretty soon," I said, hearing more footsteps in the front hall. "It's a crime scene. A forensics team is going to descend on the whole house. The medical examiner is no doubt on his way. And a homicide detective will show up to take charge of the case."

"That would be me," said a squarely built plainclothesman who stood on the edge of the living room. "I'm Detective Lieutenant Meyer Golden. I recognize Miss Nash from her movies." He glanced at me. "And you're . . . ?"

"Stewart Hoag, also known as Mister Merilee Nash as of ten o'clock this morning."

"Is that so? Congratulations."

"Thank you."

He narrowed his eyes at me. "Didn't I see you on the cover of *Time* a few months ago, Stu?"

"You may have. And make it Hoagy."

"Hoagy's a major new American novelist," Merilee said.

"Well, that would explain it."

Lulu climbed out of Phoebe's lap and ambled over to Lieutenant Golden, her tail thumping. He bent down and patted her.

"The short-legged one is Lulu," I said, glancing over at Phoebe. "And the long-legged one is—"

"I'm Merilee's cousin, Phoebe Singleton," she spoke up. "Or I should say Trowbridge, since the divorce has been finalized and I intend to use my maiden name. Junior is—make that was—my ex-husband, and this is my house for the time being. It's been my intention to sell it as soon as possible."

"I'm sorry for your loss," he said to her.

"Thank you, Lieutenant Golden."

Golden had salt-and-pepper hair, warm, sympathetic dark brown eyes, and a nose that had been broken a few times. His taste in clothing ran from awful to hideous—a cocoa-brown double knit suit with superwide lapels, a pale green polyester shirt, a red-and-white floral tie that was wide enough to double as a lobster bib, and a pair of garish platform-heeled shoes that were worthy of Disco Dan Ford, the Minnesota Twins outfielder who'd been more renowned for his outlandish footwear than his slugging percentage.

And if the name Meyer Golden sounds familiar to you, it's because ten years later, he was the hero cop who caught Briefcase Bob, the notorious subway serial killer who'd terrorized the city for an entire summer.

"Any idea what your ex-husband was doing here?" he asked Phoebe.

"Retrieving some clothes and other personal things. He phoned me yesterday to ask me if that would be okay. I'd said it would be."

"He still had a key to the place?"

"Yes, he did."

"And where has he been living since you took possession of the house?"

"In a suite at the Sherry-Netherland Hotel."

Golden excused himself and went upstairs to have a look at Junior's body, returned a moment later, and stood there at the foot of the stairs looking us over for a moment before he gestured to me with his chin to join him. I did, Lulu trailing close behind me. He led me past the kitchen to the entry hall. "The TV news crews will be swarming this place like wild animals in less than an hour. This one's going to get ugly. I've only been here ten minutes, and I can already tell it has the makings of an ulcer case. The chief of detectives will be all over me to crack it fast. So, listen, one fellow to another, can you run it for me quick?"

"Sure thing." I liked Golden. He wasn't gruff or intimidating. Acted more like a regular guy, which I was quite certain he wasn't. He wouldn't have been handed this case if he were. "Junior was a globe-trotter who was seldom around. He was also a major philanderer. Phoebe decided she'd had enough. She teaches at the Brearley School, plays the violin, reads poetry. She's sensitive, bordering on fragile."

"Not a jet-setter, in other words."

"Not greedy, either. She didn't hold him up for half of his two-hundred-million-dollar fortune—just a million dollars and this house, which, as she mentioned, she intends to sell. Workmen have been sprucing it up, so she's been staying with a friend of hers who teaches at Brearley. Did you speak to the two women in the kitchen?"

"Just briefly."

"Pippa Trowbridge, who's Phoebe's mother and Merilee's aunt, is the editor of SHE magazine and a total dragon lady. Phoebe doesn't get along with her at all. I don't think anyone does. Siena Bing is a top Millionaire's Row Realtor who's handling the sale of this place. Phoebe practically begged us to have a look at it before we leave on our one-week honeymoon in Vermont this afternoon. We'll be looking for a place, and Siena told her this one's so prime that it will probably be sold by the time we get back. Phoebe was giving us the grand tour. When we made it to the master suite, we found Junior dead on his dressing room floor with an ultra-expensive Claude Dozorme steak knife buried in his left eye. He smells as if he's been there for a while."

Golden nodded. "Eighteen to twenty-four hours, judging by his stage of rigor. The medical examiner will narrow it down. Is anyone else here?"

"Just Lulu, whom you've already met."

She let out a yip. He grinned at her, picked her up, and got his nose licked. "Say, her breath . . ."

"She has unusual eating habits."

"What does she eat, dead fish?"

"You, Lieutenant, are a first-rate detective."

The weary, heavyset medical examiner arrived, with his assistant in tow lugging two medical bags.

"Hiya, Bob," said Golden. "Third-floor master bedroom dressing room."

"Righto," he said, trudging his way toward the stairs.

Two station wagons pulled up out front next, and four men wearing forensics squad jackets piled out, gathering up their gear.

"Any idea who else has keys to this place?" Golden asked me.

"Pippa does. Siena does. And I imagine the cleaning lady, who comes in three times a week from Rockaway, does. Maybe a handyman or painter has a set until he finishes up. Siena would know."

"She's quite a dish."

"Yes, she is. Are you single, Lieutenant?"

He nodded. "It hasn't been easy to find a woman who'll put up with what I do for a living, although lately I've been seeing more and more of a pole dancer who calls herself Abraxas."

"Sounds exotic."

"Her real name is Abigail Kaminsky. She's the only Jewish pole dancer in the five boroughs. Makes three times as much money in a week as I do."

"You should marry her."

"We're getting pretty seriously involved. It could happen."

The forensics squad came trooping in now with their gear.

"Afternoon, Lieutenant," one of them said. "Whattaya need?"

"Polaroids of the body in the master suite dressing room. Once Bob's removed him, dust every inch of the suite for fingerprints. Collect every hair you can find in and on the bed. Make a top-to-bottom search of the house for breaking and entering, doors and windows. You know the drill."

And off they went.

Golden headed back toward the kitchen and living room. "I'll have to ask all of you to vacate the premises," he said in a raised voice. "This entire house is now a sealed crime scene."

"Of course," Siena said.

"And I'll need your contact information," he said to Phoebe. "Where I'll be able to find you, say, tomorrow morning. I should have the autopsy results from the medical examiner and findings from the forensics people by then. I'll also have a lot of questions to ask you."

Phoebe's eyes widened slightly in fear.

"You should have a lawyer present when he questions you," Pippa said to her.

"She certainly has a right to counsel, but I wouldn't call it necessary. I'm still in the early stages of collecting information."

Pippa glared at him. "Lieutenant Golden, I have a great deal of influence in this city. In fact, Bob Morgenthau, the Manhattan district attorney, is a personal friend. I've just spoken to him on the phone. He assures me you're a top homicide man. You'd better be, because if you don't find out what happened to Junior as soon as humanly possible, I'll make absolutely certain that you're taken off the case. Do we understand each other?"

"No, I don't believe we do, Mrs. Trowbridge," he said calmly. "I do my job well because I'm thorough and careful, so kindly take your stiletto heel off of my neck and let me do it. Do we understand each other?"

"People don't talk to me that way!" Pippa fumed.

"And yet I just did," he said, which managed to shut her up. I was liking him more and more. He turned to Phoebe and said, "Where would that steak knife have been stored?"

"In the top drawer to the left of the stove," Phoebe replied. "It was one of a set of eight that fit snugly in a lovely wooden box. One of my college friends gave it to us as a wedding present."

"Phoebe will be staying with us tonight, Lieutenant," Merilee interjected. "That's where you'll find her tomorrow morning." She gave him our address on Charlton Street as well as both of our phone numbers.

Golden jotted them down in a small notepad. "You're going to be swarmed by the tabloid media, I'm sorry to say," he warned Phoebe. "And, Miss Nash, since you're her cousin, I'm afraid you'll be hip-deep in it yourself. You, too, Hoagy."

Lulu let out a moan.

He frowned at her. "What's wrong with her?"

"She doesn't like to feel left out."

"What, she understands what people say?"

"As long as it's not in French."

"Why is that?"

"She doesn't speak French."

Golden peered at me. "You're . . . a bit off-center, aren't you?"

"I'm a writer. We're all off-center."

"I'll station a couple of patrol cars outside of the Charlton house within an hour."

"The house is in my parents' name, and our phone numbers are unlisted," Merilee pointed out.

"That may buy you a bit of time, but the tabloids will catch up with you soon. They're relentless. Okay, now would be a good time for everyone to clear out of here," he said, raising his voice for the benefit of Pippa and Siena. To us, he said, "I'll be happy to give you folks a ride home."

"We can catch a cab," I said.

"Nope. Not going to happen."

"Thank you, Lieutenant," Phoebe said softly.

Pippa and Siena lived walking distance away and left together, Pippa glaring at Golden one last time as she went out the door. She had a youthful stride for a woman in her fifties that went along with her youthful, chemically enhanced face. Siena looked defeated and downcast. Her hottest listing was now off-limits. It would also become known as the site of a notorious celebrity murder. A lot of prospective buyers don't like to live in such houses. They attract gawkers.

While we put on our coats, Lieutenant Golden made a quick trip upstairs to talk to the medical examiner and forensics team. Then he came back down, and we headed out the front door. Merilee and Phoebe got in the back seat of Golden's beat-up Ford Crown Victoria cruiser. I sat up front with the lieutenant. Lulu curled up in between us, her tail thumping happily. For some reason, she loved to ride in police cars.

It was mid-afternoon and the sun was shining. Merilee had her arm comfortingly around Phoebe, who rested her head on her shoulder. We rode in silence, Golden glancing at them in his rearview mirror from time to time. My sense was that he was trying to get a read on Phoebe. When we arrived at the Charlton house, there were indeed two police cars parked in front. There was no sign of any tabloid reporters or TV news crews yet, but I had no doubt that Golden was right. They'd show up before long.

As Merilee and Phoebe got out of the cruiser, I said, "I'll join you in a sec. Just want to mention something to the lieutenant."

"Okay, darling." Merilee unlocked the front door, and they went inside.

Golden sat there shaking his head. "You'd expect a world-class adventurer to die high atop Mount Everest, not on a closet floor with a steak knife in his eyeball." He glanced over at me. "So what do you want to tell me?"

"That I was acquainted with Junior. We were classmates at Harvard, and we both belonged to the Racquet and Tennis Club."

He raised his eyebrows. "Very exclusive."

"Also the Lunch Club."

"The Lunch Club. That's the secret society of giants in their fields who meet regularly around a big table to discuss weighty topics, am I right?"

"Yes, you are."

"How did you get into that?"

"I was invited. I suppose my book made an impression on someone."

"I see. And you're telling me this because . . . ?"

"I didn't want you to find out on your own that I knew Junior. I thought it might appear as if I had something to hide. I didn't. I don't."

"Okay." He sat there studying me. "What did you think of him?"

"I thought he was a restless soul who was searching for something to give his life meaning and never finding it. He was a compulsive womanizer. He also moved with a pretty wild crowd when he was in England. Group sex, drugs . . ."

"And how do you know that?"

"We had a lot of similar experiences. I wasn't always a successful author. I plunged headfirst into the punk scene when I moved to New York in the late seventies. Dropped acid, snorted coke, tore around on a Norton Commando getting in and out of all kinds of trouble. My girlfriend in those days was a wild, crazy poet named Reggie Aintree."

"Am I going to find out you have a sheet?"

"I'll let that come as a surprise to you."

"One more question, Hoagy. Did Junior and Phoebe seem like a match to you? What I mean is, she doesn't strike me as the adventuresome type."

"She's not, and no, they didn't. But she's beautiful, classy, and smart. A real catch."

"I agree. And she's about to become a real catch again. Unless . . ."

"Unless what?"

"Unless she's the one who murdered him."

CHAPTER FOUR

Lulu headed straight for the refrigerator and sat and stared at it, which was her way of reminding me I'd promised her an anchovy treat. She prefers them cold because the oil clings better. After I fed it to her, she climbed her way up the stairs, one by one by one, while I phoned Rocco at the garage to tell him that we would not be picking up the Land Rover that day. I rescheduled it for the following week and assured him I understood there was a significant financial penalty involved.

Merilee was getting Phoebe settled in the guest room on the fourth floor. I hung up my wedding suit, pausing to gaze at it so I'd never forget it commemorated one of the most special days of my life. Then I changed into a Sex Pistols T-shirt, aged jeans, an even more aged navy blue turtleneck sweater, and my black high-top Converse Chuck Taylor All Stars. Hey, on my wedding day, I was going to wear whatever the hell I wanted. Then I headed upstairs to the guest room.

Merilee, who'd changed out of her wedding dress into one of my old flannel shirts and a pair of jeans, had made up the guest bed for Phoebe and loaned her a pair of sweatpants, a Miss Porter's School sweatshirt, and thick wool socks. Phoebe was stretched out on the bed, looking utterly drained. Lulu had curled up on her tummy to comfort her.

"Well, don't you two look nice and cozy," I said.

"This is so sweet of you guys," she said, her eyes tearing up.

"Nonsense," Merilee said. "It's our pleasure. Can I get you anything? A cup of cocoa? A Valium? Two Valiums?"

"What I'd really like is to see Barry. Would you mind if I invited him over?"

"Of course not. Invite him over for dinner. I can thaw some four-alarm chili. We've got plenty of beer. Ask him to stop by after he closes his office for the day. The phone's right there on the nightstand. We'll leave you in peace."

Or at least two of us did. Lulu stayed curled up on Phoebe. She always seemed to know when she was needed.

Downstairs in the kitchen, Merilee pulled two containers of her primo four-alarm chili out of the freezer, then took a deep breath and dialed the phone. We had two lines on the kitchen phone, one for each of us. Since hers was lit up—Phoebe had evidently gotten through to Barry—she used mine.

"It's Merilee, Aunt Pippa," my new bride said in a clear, confident voice. "I wanted you to know that Phoebe is safe and snug. I've just put her to bed . . . No, the tabloids don't know she's here. No one does, except for Lieutenant Golden and you . . . Please don't take offense, but no, I don't think it would be a good idea for you to come over. She needs to stay calm right now, and calm isn't exactly what the two of you exude together. You're more like a tsunami . . . That wasn't intended as a criticism. I simply wanted to let you know she's fine and I'll speak to you in the morning, okay? Goodbye." She hung up before Pippa could get out another word, took a deep breath, and let it out slowly.

I gazed at her in admiration. "Well handled, Mrs. Hoag."

"You're not actually going to call me that from now on, are you?"

"Wasn't planning on it. Not unless you want me to. Would you prefer Buttercup? Okay, ow, that hurt."

Phoebe called out to Merilee from upstairs. While Merilee went up to see what she wanted, I took a poker to the coals in the fireplace, which were still glowing from our post-wedding champagne celebration. I revived them with the bellows, a page from yesterday's *Times,* and some kindling, then set two logs on the grate. They were crackling in no time. I fetched two small glasses and the bottle of twenty-one-year-old Balvenie single malt Scotch from the kitchen, flopped down on the sofa before the fire, and poured two generous jolts while I waited for Merilee to come back downstairs.

"Is Barry coming over?" I asked her when she snuggled next to me with a weary sigh.

"His office closes at six. He'll be here as soon as he can get away." We clinked glasses and drank, both of us savoring the smooth warmth of the precious Scotch.

"Well, this sure has been some wedding day, hasn't it?" she said. "It's not as if I was ever going to forget any of it, but now it's a day that will live in infamy. I just wish we were on our way to the Enchanted Cottage."

"Merilee . . . ?"

"Yes, darling?"

"Let's not buy Phoebe's town house."

"Let's not," she agreed. "We'll never be able to forget what we saw."

I sipped my Scotch. "You don't suppose she killed him, do you?"

"Who, Phoebe? I'd find that hard to believe. She's such a gentle soul."

"Exactly."

"Meaning?"

"Those are the sort who really lose it when they lose it."

Merilee studied me over the rim of her glass. "She got the divorce settlement that she wanted. Why would she stab Junior in the eyeball with a steak knife?"

"I dunno, how about because she hated his guts?"

"I don't buy it. Besides, she's in love with Barry now. Her face lights up at the mere mention of his name."

I topped off our Scotch glasses. "At least we have a bit of time to unwind and make out in front of the fire, just like we did that first night I stayed here, remember?" I kissed her gently, getting lost in her green eyes. "I played you my Alberta Hunter and Erroll Garner albums. I even got to second base."

"Second base? Hell, you slid headfirst into home plate, Writer Boy."

"Why, Merilee Gilbert Nash. You've gotten quite ribald since you've become a married woman."

"Shut up and kiss me some more."

"Bossy, too." We kissed—a long, lingering kiss—before I said, "Junior's killer was with him when he let himself into the house. Or they'd made arrangements to meet there. A lover whom he intended to break up with. Or a friend with whom he was having a bitter disagreement."

"What kind of bitter disagreement?"

"Hell, I don't know. I'm just thinking out loud."

"I'm too tired to think out loud. Or in total silence. Can we just sit here and hold each other until Barry shows up?"

Which is what we did. Soon, we dozed off in each other's arms. A log burned through and collapsed from the grate in a cascade of sparks, startling both of us awake. I got up and fed the fire with fresh logs.

That was when someone used the old-fashioned door knocker on the front door. I glanced at Grandfather's Benrus. It was just past 6:30. Lulu came scampering down the stairs, barking her head off. She'd become very territorial.

I went to the door and called out, "Who is it?"

"Barry Zallinger," a voice responded.

I opened the door and let him in, glancing around for the tabloid media lemmings. There was no sign of them yet. Nonetheless, Lieutenant Golden was a careful man. Two patrol cars were parked across the street, four doors down, just in case our house suddenly became a media attraction.

The new love of Phoebe's stood there in the entry hall rubbing his hands together, his face flushed from the cold. Dashingly handsome Barry was not. He was a gawky eye doctor in his late thirties with stooped shoulders. His sandy-colored hair was thinning on top, his chin was weak, and his Adam's apple rated as beyond significant. I helped him off with his quilted down jacket and hung it on a hook for him. He wore a gray lambswool V-neck sweater over a light blue button-down shirt, permanent press tan slacks, and a pair of Clarks Wallabees.

"Hi, I'm Barry," he said bashfully, treating me to a limp, chilly handshake. Honestly? I couldn't think of anyone who was less like Junior if I tried.

"Stewart Hoag," I said. "Make it Hoagy. The short one is Lulu, and that semi-attractive blonde who's lazing on the sofa is—"

"You don't have to tell me," he said with a goofy grin. "I'm a huge fan of your work, Miss Nash."

"Call me Merilee, please. Phoebe's waiting for you in my old room up on the fourth floor."

"I understand from Phoebe that you got married today. Congratulations!"

"Thank you," I said. "It's ended up not being a very festive day, what with finding Junior dead on the floor of his dressing room. But, in the immortal words of Ozzie Nelson, it was just one of those little surprises that make life so interesting."

"Come on upstairs," Merilee said. "Phoebe's anxious to see you."

When Barry walked into the bedroom, Phoebe sat up in bed and held her arms out to him, tears streaming down her face. "I'm so glad you're here."

He sat on the bed and took her in his arms. "Of course I'm here."

"H-he had a knife in his eye and dried blood all over his face. It was so awful."

"Try not to think about it," he said, hugging her tightly.

"We're going to have some four-alarm chili for dinner if you can stay," Merilee said to him. "There's beer, wine . . ."

"Sounds great," he said as Lulu circled around him, sniffing the cuffs of his trousers and his shoes. Particularly his shoes.

"Why's she doing that?" he wondered.

"Couldn't tell you," I said. "She doesn't share information with us."

We left the two of them alone and went back downstairs. Lulu came plop-plopping down, too, not so much to give them their privacy but because she wanted her half can of 9Lives mackerel.

"He seems like a nice guy," I said as I opened Lulu's can in the kitchen.

"He does," Merilee agreed. "They seem genuinely fond of each other. And a gentle soul is just what she needs right now."

We sat back down in front of the fire, and they joined us a few minutes later. Phoebe sat close to Barry and clutched his hand. He stroked her hair.

Lulu had polished off her dinner and now needed to go for a walk. I knew this because she'd started scratching at the front door.

I said, "If you'll excuse me for a few minutes, Lulu has to take a walk. When a puppy needs to walk, it's nonnegotiable."

"Care for some company?" Barry asked, to my surprise.

"Sure, if you'd like. But wouldn't you rather stay here with Phoebe?"

"I feel like some fresh air. Been cooped up in my office with patients all day."

Phoebe squeezed his hand. "Go ahead. You should get to know Hoagy. You two will like each other."

He put his down jacket back on while I put on my shearling coat and gloves. I offered to loan Barry a pair, but he assured me he was fine. Lulu circled eagerly, yipping and yapping when I grabbed her leash and attached it to her collar.

It had gotten windier out. The two strategically placed patrol cars were still there, but, happily, there was still no sign of the tabloid lemmings. It was taking them a while to figure out where Phoebe was hiding out. But it wouldn't be long before they descended upon us. They'd been handed a grisly multimillionaire celebrity murder, complete with an Oscar-winning movie star attached to it.

Lulu made her usual stops as we worked our way slowly along Charlton toward Varick.

"I don't have many male friends, as it happens," Barry said, clearing his throat uncomfortably. "In fact, I don't have any. I don't know why that is. My office staff is all women. My chamber music group is all women. Would you mind if I ask you something, guy to guy, in total confidence?"

"Fire away. Whatever's on your mind will stay between us."

"Great, thanks," he said before he took a deep breath and blurted out, "Is it possible for a man to be in love with two women at the same time?"

Right away, I felt my stomach tighten. "Are you telling me there's another woman in your life besides Phoebe?"

He considered his response carefully. "No . . . I wouldn't put it that way exactly. I love Phoebe more than any woman I've ever known. I cherish every minute we're together and truly can't believe she feels that way about me."

"So what are we talking about? Or should I say, who are we talking about?"

"Elvia," he confessed.

"And who is Elvia?"

"One of my opticians. She performs the basic eye tests. Asks you to read the eye chart and so on. She's been with me for four years. She's thirty-six, married, has two kids, and lives in Teaneck with her husband, Pete. He's a certified public accountant. Has an office out there. Prepares tax returns for retail establishments, private individuals, and—"

"Okay, and getting back to Elvia?"

"We started having sex two years ago. Her sex life with Pete had become dormant. My own sex life had become, well, nonexistent, and she's very attractive. It started out innocently enough. We'd grab a sandwich at the neighborhood deli and talk about the office. Then, gradually, we moved on to more personal things, such as her confessing how sexually frustrated she was. Before I knew it, we started having nooners in her sister's apartment two, three times a week. Her sister lives in the East Fifties, not far from my office. She's an executive secretary, loves Elvia, and will do anything for her. Her husband's an executive with the Metropolitan Transit Authority. We use their guest room. They have no kids."

"Does anyone in your office know?"

"No. We've been very discreet."

"How many people do you employ?"

"Six."

"All women, you said?"

"All women."

"No offense, Barry, but if you've been having nooners with Elvia several times a week for two years, everyone in your office knows."

He looked at me in surprise. "Do you really think so?"

"No, I really know so. Trust me. Getting back to where this tawdry tale began, are you telling me that you love both Phoebe and Elvia?"

"That's what I don't know. I yearn for Elvia. The sex is amazing. From the very start, we just fused together like it was meant to be. But she's a married woman. She has Pete and the kids to think of. And I don't want to break up her home."

"And what about Phoebe?"

"When Phoebe spends the night at my place, the sex is beyond anything I've ever dreamt of. She gives herself to me so completely and trustingly."

"Which must mean she doesn't know about Elvia."

"That's correct."

"Does Elvia know about Phoebe?"

"That's a no."

"In other words, you're cheating on both of them and are a total louse."

"I don't think of myself that way," he said, wounded by my reproach. "I'm totally in love with Phoebe. I'd give anything to marry her. But I also can't imagine not being with Elvia. I'm all torn up inside. I don't know what the hell to do. That's why I wanted to talk to you. I was hoping you might have some advice."

Lulu came to a halt and sat down.

"Why is she doing that?" Barry asked me.

"She's ready to cross Charlton and work her way back home." Which was what we did, pausing as Lulu made her regular stops. "You want my advice? Okay, sure. Let me start by asking you something. Do you intend to continue sleeping with Elvia if you and Phoebe get married?"

"I don't see how I can. Not in good conscience."

"Are you going to tell Phoebe about Elvia?"

"God no. She'd dump me in two seconds."

"And deservedly so."

"I gather you don't think too much of me." He sounded wounded again.

"I'm no angel. Before I met Merilee, I broke the hearts of three terrific women by behaving like an even bigger jerk than you are. But if you want to clean up the mess you've made of your love life, then you have to break it off with Elvia right away."

He gulped, his huge Adam's apple bobbing up and down. "How?"

"Fire her."

"But she's been an exemplary employee for four years."

"In which case, she'll have no trouble finding another job in no time, preferably in Teaneck. How many opticians do you employ?"

"Two. It keeps the patient flow moving along."

"Perfect. Fire her and keep the other one. Tell Elvia you have to pare down the size of your practice because all you do is work and you're burning out. Fire one of your front desk people, too, so that it won't look like you're doing what you're really doing."

Barry considered this in silence for a moment. "Fire her? For real?"

"For real. I guarantee you, once the two of you no longer work together, every day the flame of passion will flicker and you'll stop yearning for her. She's another man's wife, Barry, and you have a beautiful, sensitive woman who's in love with you. Fire Elvia. If you don't, then you don't deserve Phoebe. Even if you do fire her, I'm still not sure you deserve Phoebe."

He shot a hurt look at me. "You sound pissed."

"I am pissed. It's been one hell of a rotten day, and you've just made it worse. You asked me for my advice. I've given it to you. Fire Elvia. And while you're at it, tighten up your wig."

"Tighten up my what?"

"I guess you weren't a Steppenwolf fan in their glory years. Translation: Get your head on straight." I glared at him. "Are you hearing me?"

"I-I'm hearing you."

"You'd better be."

◆

"Do I know how to show you a boffo wedding night or what?"

"You'll get no complaints from me, Hubby," Merilee said.

We were in bed eating bowls of chili on dinner trays, washing it down with that second bottle of 1966 Dom Pérignon I'd bought, and watching *The Palm Beach Story,* our favorite Preston Sturges screwball comedy, on our videocassette recorder. Lulu was stretched out between us, her tail thumping happily. She loves the Ale and Quail Club.

When Barry and I had returned from our walk, we discovered that Phoebe had taken a Valium and was fast asleep in bed. He'd elected not to stay for dinner, which I considered a wise choice, though he did go upstairs to kiss her good night.

"Yet, somehow, I thought the three of us would be having a more exciting evening," I said.

"This is plenty exciting for me, sir. Tell me, did you get a good feeling about Barry when you took your walk?"

I didn't respond.

She reached for the remote and paused the movie. "Hello . . . ?"

"I promised him I wouldn't repeat a word of what he told me, but I refuse to start our marriage by keeping ugly secrets from you."

"Oh, dear, I don't like the sound of this at all." She looked at me fretfully. "What is it, darling?"

"He's not the kindly soul Phoebe thinks he is. He not only started having an affair with his married optician, Elvia, two years ago, but he's continued to have nooners with her while he's been carrying on with Phoebe. He wanted to know if I thought it was possible for a man to love two women at the same time. He truly loves Phoebe, or so he claims, but he yearns for Elvia. Yearns."

"Why that sneaky, horny jerk! And poor Phoebe thinks he's so sweet and sensitive. What did you tell him?"

"That if he intends to pursue a serious relationship with Phoebe, he has to break it off with Elvia."

"Do you think he will?"

"Honestly? No. See above, re: yearns."

"Phoebe doesn't have very good taste in men, does she? Not like me."

"Why, Merilee, that's the second nicest thing you've said to me since the night we met."

"What's the nicest?"

"'If we're not naked together in my bed in the next five minutes, I'm going to consider this evening a complete failure.'"

She reached over and stroked my face. "Have I told you recently that I love you?"

"You've never told me you love me."

"Liar. Shut up and kiss me."

"If I'd known you were going to be such a bossy wife, I would have had to reconsider this whole thing," I said before I kissed her—and then proceeded to do a whole lot more.

After all, it was our wedding night.

CHAPTER FIVE

Lulu woke me before dawn to take her out for her morning walk. I stirred and got into my Sex Pistols T-shirt, old turtleneck, torn jeans, and socks in the dark—although there's actually no such thing as total darkness in the city that never sleeps—and padded downstairs without awakening Merilee. I turned on the vestibule light so I could tie the laces on my Chuck Taylors, climb into my shearling coat, and hook Lulu's leash to her collar as she let out yips and yaps of increasing urgency.

And out the door we went, Lulu stopping at the first tree out front to pee as I stood there yawning. It was a raw winter morning. A police car was parked across the street, but there was still no sign of TV news crews or tabloid photographers. All remained quiet.

After Lulu had made three more stops, she decided she wanted to cross the street, so we did. When it comes to her walks, Lulu is just like Lola in *Damn Yankees*—whatever Lulu wants, Lulu gets. As we strolled along, a battered Crown Victoria pulled up alongside us.

Lieutenant Meyer Golden lowered his window and said, "Hop in."

"Don't you ever sleep?" I asked him as Lulu and I got in the front seat.

"I do, but the medical examiner doesn't. He and his entire team pulled an all-nighter on Junior Singleton's autopsy. He called me with the results at five o'clock. We need to talk."

"In that case, come on inside. I'll make us some espresso."

He was wearing the same wide-lapeled cocoa-brown double knit suit he'd worn yesterday—unless, God help him, he owned two—with a lavender polyester shirt and lemon-yellow lobster-bib necktie. He'd grabbed the morning papers from a twenty-four-hour newsstand and handed them to me after he pulled up in front of the house and parked. *The Daily News* had gone with a SOCIETY SLAYING front-page screamer headline. *The Post* opted for WHO KILLED JUNIOR? The below-the-fold page-one headline on the somnambulistic *Times* read: GLOBAL ADVENTURER SINGLETON FOUND DEAD IN FORMER EAST SIDE HOME. Not my idea of pleasant early morning reading, although I did find it satisfying to know that Junior's murder would infuriate George Steinbrenner, whose rehiring of the odious Billy Martin as manager of the Bronx Bombers had been bumped from the front page of all three newspapers.

By the time I let us into the house, there was a light on in the kitchen, and a semi-awake Merilee, wearing a cashmere robe and shearling moccasins, was padding around, starting to make the espresso, her waist-length golden hair pulled up in a bun.

"Good morning, Lieutenant," she said, which elicited nothing more than a grim nod in response. "Don't you ever sleep?"

I said, "He does, but the medical examiner doesn't. He said we need to talk, so I'm guessing it's pretty important or he wouldn't be here this early." I plopped the newspapers down on the kitchen table and got busy putting down Lulu's breakfast, which she devoured hungrily.

Merilee scanned the papers with dread. "Drat, my name is mentioned in paragraph three of the *Times*."

"It was bound to happen."

As soon as the espresso was ready, she urged Golden to have a seat at the table, presented him with the first cup of espresso, and urged him to have at it. The second cup was for me, and I required no urging. As Golden and I took grateful sips of our piping-hot caffeinated gold, she made two more cups and took small sips of hers as she carried the fourth cup up to Phoebe in the guest room. Golden finished off his espresso and sat there in uneasy silence until Merilee returned.

"Did she get any sleep?" I asked her.

"Not a lot. She looks devastated. But she'll be down as soon as she gets her morning jolt of caffeine and splashes some water on her face."

We started hearing cars pull up out front, van doors slide open and shut, and raised urgent voices. The house's old-fashioned door knocker went knock-knock-knock repeatedly.

"She's been found," Golden said, glancing out the kitchen window. "Those damned tabloid reporters are like bounty hunters. They never quit until they catch their prey. I'll double the police presence here, but it's still going to be an ugly day." He glanced at the phone. "May I . . . ?"

"Please do," I said, swiftly closing the wooden shutters over the kitchen and living room windows. I also threw the bolt on the front door and closed the door to the vestibule, which deadened the knock-knock-knocking a bit.

Golden phoned in that he needed more patrol cars at the Charlton Street address. His voice was clipped and authoritative, although a lot of what he said was cop speak, as in I didn't understand half of it. I did make out the word "barricades."

Phoebe came downstairs wearing the same Miss Porter's sweatshirt and sweatpants as last evening. Merilee hadn't been exaggerating. She looked devastated. Disoriented. Blown away. Freaked out. Zonked. Take your pick.

"Good morning," I said, forcing a smile onto my face as she set her empty cup in the sink.

She joined us at the table. "It . . . sounds as if we're being invaded," she said in a soft, halting voice.

"Only because we are, but the lieutenant has called in the cavalry. Not to worry. We'll get through this."

I could already hear sirens in the distance. The man definitely had pull.

"It's not even seven o'clock," Phoebe said. "Why are you here so early, Lieutenant?"

"I got a call two hours ago from the medical examiner," Golden answered apologetically. "I have some important information to share. It concerns your ex-husband's autopsy results."

Her eyes widened slightly. "What is it?"

He pulled out his notepad from the chest pocket of his suit and cleared his throat. "I'll just go ahead and run his findings for you, if you don't mind."

"Go right ahead," Merilee said.

"The time of death was approximately eighteen hours before you folks found him yesterday, shortly after one P.M. That means he was killed at approximately seven P.M. on Monday. The wound to his eyeball from that steak knife was delivered with considerable force. His killer was strong enough to drive the blade deep into his skull."

"Does that mean his killer was a man?" I asked.

"Not necessarily. A strong woman could have done it. There was no sign that a violent struggle took place.

He wasn't scratched up or bruised. No defensive wounds were found, such as someone else's blood under his fingernails." Golden paused, clearing his throat uneasily. "But the medical examiner was in for something of a shock when he conducted a thorough search of Junior's body."

Phoebe peered at him warily. "What sort of a shock?"

"You'd better brace yourself," he responded, "because it's a doozy. He discovered what's known as a Kaposi sarcoma lesion in the crease on the back of Junior's left knee. His team immediately ran an antigen/antibody blood test on him, and I'm sorry to say that your ex-husband was HIV positive. He had the AIDS virus, for which there is no cure, as I'm sure you know."

Phoebe drew her breath in, stunned. "Are you kidding me?"

"I wish I were."

Merilee and I gaped at each other in stunned silence.

"No one knows about this yet," Golden hastened to point out. "We haven't released the results of Junior's autopsy to a soul." He cleared his throat uneasily again. "Phoebe, I realize that this is a very personal question, and I take no pleasure in asking it, but when did you last have sex with your ex-husband?"

She reddened. "It was . . . about two months ago, I guess."

"Forgive me, but was it unprotected?"

"Yes, it was. I'd filed for the divorce by then. He'd just returned from London, and we were reminiscing over a glass of wine and, well, one thing led to another. That was our very last time together. I suppose it was our way of saying goodbye. It was a-a very emotional experience for me."

"So you'd estimate it took place eight weeks ago?"

"Yes."

"Could it have been seven weeks?"

Phoebe flared at him. "It's not as if I marked it on my calendar."

"Could it have been seven?" he repeated stubbornly.

"Yes, I suppose."

"In that case, I would highly recommend you get the antigen blood test as a precaution. One of our medical technicians can administer it to you right here today. According to the medical examiner, twenty-five percent of HIV-positive cases show flu-like symptoms within two weeks. After another week, the number goes up to 50 percent. Ninety-nine percent of cases show up within forty-three days, as in just over six weeks. Some people who have contracted the virus are asymptomatic, which means they don't even know they have it."

"I feel fine."

"You should still get tested, Phoebe," Merilee said to her. "Just to play it safe."

Phoebe's mouth tightened. "Okay . . ."

"I was told that the AIDS virus is contracted in one of two ways," Golden went on. "By having unprotected sexual intercourse or by an intravenous drug user sharing a needle with someone who has the virus. A sizable percentage of those who've contracted it are gay men. The Centers for Disease Control have no idea why. At this point, they're still in the learning stage."

"And dragging their feet, according to every gay actor and dancer I know," Merilee said disapprovingly.

"I wouldn't know about that," he said, carefully sidestepping what was becoming a raging controversy in the arts world. Also in the minority community, where the percentage of incarcerated Black men who had the virus was becoming alarmingly high. "Forgive me for asking, Phoebe, but was Junior bisexual?"

"You mean did he sleep with men as well as women?" Phoebe let out a pained sigh. "I have no idea. All I can tell you is that he had more than his share of wild experiences whenever he was in London. He lived for wild experiences."

"Might that have included shooting heroin?"

"I have no idea."

Golden thumbed his jaw thoughtfully. "I understand he had numerous affairs. It's possible he had sex with a woman who'd picked up the virus from her husband or boyfriend but didn't know it yet. Had you seen him recently?"

Phoebe shook her head.

"So you wouldn't know if he appeared to be in good health or not."

I said, "He looked perfectly fine to me when I saw him last week at the Lunch Club."

"Good to know," Golden said. "Phoebe, your housekeeper, Katie Healey, told us she saw him last week, too, when he dropped by the house to pick up some clothes. He was with a heavyset, well-dressed British friend. She thought Junior appeared fit and healthy, too."

The kitchen phone rang. It was Merilee's line. She answered it and immediately made a face. "Good morning to you, too, Aunt Pippa." She punched a button on the phone to put it on speaker.

"I wish to speak with Phoebe, Merilee." Pippa's voice came through loud and clear.

Phoebe shook her head no.

"I'm afraid she's still asleep. She was awfully exhausted."

"Then tell her to call me when she gets up. I want her to come home."

"She is home. She's staying with us."

"In case you've forgotten, dear, I happen to be her mother."

"You also happen to make her very uncomfortable. She's in a fragile state right now. The last thing she needs is to be bullied by you."

"Don't you talk to me that way, young lady!"

"I'll talk to you any way I feel like talking to you. And don't try to bully me because you'll be wasting your time. I walked off a $40 million-dollar Kubrick picture because I would not be bullied. The project got shelved, and he couldn't raise the money for another picture for three years. I'm hanging up now." And she did—before Pippa could say another word.

That reminds me, in case I didn't mention it before: Don't mess with Merilee.

"Thank you," Phoebe said to her quietly.

"It was my pleasure," Merilee assured her as we heard angry voices outside. The cops had arrived and were beginning to wage a turf battle with the tabloid press.

Golden glanced through his notepad. "We've questioned the neighbors, by the way. No one saw Junior or anyone else enter the house at the approximate time of death. Siena Bing was showing another house at the time. And the cleaning lady, Katie Healey, was home in Rockaway Beach with her daughter Bridget."

"What about your forensics team?" I asked. "Have they turned up anything helpful?"

"They found no fingerprints on the dressing room doorknob, which had been wiped clean. No hairs or other trace evidence in or on the bed, nor anywhere else in the suite. We're dealing with someone careful. But they're still searching. The master bath may reveal something." Golden glanced through his notepad. "They did find that wooden box with the matched set of eight steak knives next to the stove, as you mentioned," he said to Phoebe.

"And one is missing, I gather," Phoebe said.

"No, two are. There are only six in the box."

Phoebe blinked at him. "What on earth does that mean?"

"My guess? The killer intends to use another knife on someone else."

"You're . . . scaring me, Lieutenant," Phoebe said, her voice quavering.

"It's a scary situation, no question. But this is what I do for a living, and I'm taking it very seriously. You'll be under police protection twenty-four hours a day from now on. You mentioned that Junior had been living in a suite at the Sherry-Netherland Hotel on Fifth Avenue."

"Yes, he moved in there when I took formal possession of the house."

"The management at the Sherry-Netherland told us he seldom stayed in his suite there. Any idea where else he might have been staying?"

"None."

Golden removed a Polaroid photo from his jacket pocket. "Forensics also found this coat hanging in the entry hall closet. Can you confirm that it was his?"

It was a photo of a tan hooded duffel coat that had seen many years of wear.

"That was Junior's, all right," I said.

He peered at me. "You're sure about that?"

"Positive. I've coveted it since we were at Harvard together. It's not the apex of duffel coats, which is the one that Trevor Howard wore in *The Third Man*, but it's a real beaut. He was wearing it last week when I saw him at the Lunch Club. Did they find anything in the pockets?"

"They did, as a matter of fact. The key to his hotel suite, a bag of grape lollipops . . ." He glanced at Phoebe. "Was he a fan of grape lollipops?"

She shook her head. "I never saw him sucking on one."

". . . As well as a half-dozen crumpled phone messages from the hotel operator, all from a woman named Betty Page asking him to please call her. The word 'please' was underlined for emphasis. Do you know her?" he asked Phoebe.

"I'm afraid not."

"How did the hotel operator spell the name Betty?" I asked him.

Golden frowned at me. "What do you mean?"

"I mean, does it end with a *y* or an *ie*?"

He consulted his notepad. "An *ie,* now that you mention it. Is there some significance to that?"

"Major significance. Bettie Page was the most famous nude cheesecake model of the fifties. The Playboy Playmates were a Hugh Hefner creation. Bettie was her own creation."

"Are you suggesting Junior was seeing her?"

"Oh, heck no. She was born in the twenties. Besides, she renounced her evil ways in the late fifties, became an Evangelical Christian, and fell in with Billy Graham before she became a paranoid schizophrenic and had to be hospitalized."

"She still alive?"

"I believe so."

"How do you know so much about her, darling?" Merilee asked me.

"She's an interesting character. Writers collect interesting characters."

Golden said, "Are you suggesting that the name his caller left with the hotel operator was some kind of inside-joke pseudonym?"

"Exactly. And, whoever she was, he wasn't calling her back."

"Hmm . . ." He turned back to Phoebe. "Just to play it safe, I'd stay put here today, if I were you. Don't go out. I'll arrange for a police medical technician to stop by to administer your blood test."

"But I don't have anything to wear," she said. "I need to pick up some clothes at the apartment where I've been staying."

"In that case, we'll take you there in a patrol car and bring you right back."

"And I'll go with you," Merilee said.

"Okay, I'm outta here," Golden said, glancing at me as he started toward the vestibule. "Have a quick word with you?"

I joined him. He closed the vestibule door behind us so whatever that quick word was wouldn't be overheard by Phoebe and Merilee. Lulu let out a little yip just to let us know she was in there with us.

"Know anything about this British friend of Junior's that Katie mentioned?" he murmured.

I nodded. "I met him at the Racquet and Tennis Club about a month ago. He's an international investment broker. His name is Jon, as in Jonathan, Porterfield. Divides his time between here and Britain, where I gather that he and Junior shared some wild times together. As soon as Junior told him I was a best-selling author, he said, 'If you're looking for a 28 percent return on your investments, call me.' He gave me his card. I still have it somewhere."

"He's someone I want to talk to. And so are you."

"Talk away, I'm listening."

"As soon as this story made the TV news last night, I heard from a Connecticut State Police homicide lieutenant named Buck Mitry. He told me that he'd had reason to be in close contact with you on a murder case in a town called Oakmont three months ago. I checked him out. He's a rising star, very by the book, but he swore to me that you cracked his case for him."

"Actually, that was Lulu, not me."

"He also told me to ignore that you have a sheet." He glanced at his notepad. "Let's see . . . reckless driving, drunk and disorderly, indecent public exposure, and you threw a barstool through the front window of P.J. Clarke's."

"I told you I was a bit wild in my youth."

"There was a man sitting on the barstool at the time."

"It was my stool and he wouldn't get off."

"Straight up? I don't like working with amateurs. In fact, I don't like working with anyone. I'm a lone wolf. But you saw the headlines. This is a page-one society murder. I'm under a huge amount of pressure. My entire career is on the line here. Mitry said you're a special case. Highly perceptive, with keen insights into people and an uncanny knack for connecting the dots."

"Lieutenant, are you saying you want to partner up? Because if you are, I'll need to know two things—whether I'm going to be Starsky or Hutch, and whether you can deal with Lulu mouth breathing in your cruiser day and night."

He grimaced. "Okay, what he didn't tell me was how annoying you are."

"Really? I'd have thought it would have been the first thing he mentioned."

Golden stood there in tight silence for a long moment, narrowing his gaze at me, before he said, "I don't know what the hell I was thinking. I must be desperate. Let's just forget we had this conversation, okay?"

I shook my head. "No, not okay. Let's try a do-over. Are you saying you want my help?"

"I'm saying that someone like this Jon Porterfield will tell you things he won't tell me. Things I need to know. Can I count on you?"

"That depends. Does it work both ways?"

"How so?"

"Will you tell me what you know?"

"I'll tell you as much as I can."

"What does that mean?"

"It means I can't share sworn testimony. I won't break any rules."

"Rules are made to be broken."

"So is your nose."

"That was beneath you, Lieutenant."

"I apologize." He lowered his voice to scarcely more than a whisper. "We've talked a lot about Junior's sex life. What do you know about Phoebe's?"

I'd promised Barry I wouldn't repeat anything he told me, and if I didn't think the guy was a detestable two-timing schmuck, I'd have told Golden I had no idea. The problem was that he was a detestable two-timing shmuck who was playing fast and loose with Phoebe's fragile heart. I lowered my own voice and said, "Okay, you didn't hear this from me, but she's sleeping with a Fifth Avenue eye doctor named Barry Zallinger. He plays cello in her chamber music quartet. He's the anti-Junior. Gentle, sensitive, kind of nerdy. She's madly in love with the guy. What she doesn't know, and Barry told me in the strictest confidence, is that he's been banging his married optician, Elvia, for the past two years and still hasn't given her up. He wanted my advicc."

"Advice about what?"

"Whether it's possible to be in love with two women at the same time. He told me he loves Phoebe but yearns for Elvia."

"You figure him for a potential suspect?"

"Let's say he decided to have a talk with Junior to tell him it was his intention to marry Phoebe. Let's say Junior laughed in his face and told him to dream on. Barry didn't strike me as the violent type, but he is an eye doctor, and Junior did get stabbed in the eyeball with that steak knife. There's a certain symmetry there, if you're into symmetry."

"There's still another steak knife missing."

"Believe me, I haven't forgotten that."

"If he killed Junior, who'd be next on his list?"

"Elvia, who else? He may yearn for her, but she could queer things for him with Phoebe big time if she picked up the phone and ratted him out."

Golden mulled it over. "That's a good lead, Hoagy. It plays. But listen to me—whoever did this has already killed once and won't hesitate to kill again to protect their identity. So don't try to be a hero. I'm not Batman, you're not Robin, and Lulu isn't Alfred the Butler."

"But this is Gotham City."

He rolled his eyes. "Okay, I'll let you have that one." And with that, out the front door he went into a crush of cameramen and cops.

I returned to the kitchen just in time to devour a toasted baguette with butter and blueberry jam and savor a second steaming-hot cup of espresso.

"What were you two muttering about in there?" Merilee asked as she and Phoebe studied me curiously.

"He was wondering what I know about Jon Porterfield, Junior's British friend."

"And what do you know about him?"

"Very little. He's an international money man whom I met once at the Racquet and Tennis Club. He was eager to invest my newfound wealth for me. Even gave me his card. Golden wants me to get in touch with him. Thinks he'll be more candid with me than with the law about whom Junior's been hanging out with lately. Did you ever meet him?" I asked Phoebe.

She shook her head. "I don't recall Junior even mentioning his name."

"What's your plan for today?" I asked Merilee.

"Robert Altman's assistant left a message that he wants to have a sit-down with me, but she wasn't clear on whether he's flying in from LA today or tomorrow. It seems he thrives on spontaneity. I'd love to take a yoga class, but the lieutenant wants us to stay close to home, so Phoebe and I will practice here together after the patrolmen help us fetch some clothes for her from Meredith's apartment. And I gather that a police medical technician will be stopping by to take a blood sample from her."

"I can't wait," Phoebe said with a distinct lack of enthusiasm.

"We need to make sure that you're okay, Phoebe."

"I know," she said hollowly.

"If your phone rings, it'll probably be reporters," I said. "Let your machine take it. That goes for my phone, too. Don't answer it. I can call it and retrieve my messages remotely. My physical therapist wants me to get in a forty-five-minute swim today, so I'll be heading to the club with my lifeguard." Lulu let out an eager whoop. "And I'm going to find the business card that Jon gave me. See if I can arrange to meet with him."

But first I went upstairs, stropped Grandfather's straight razor, lathered up with my badger brush, and shaved. When I was done, I patted my face with Floris No. 89 talc. I dressed in my gray cheviot wool suit with a navy blue Viyella shirt, a yellow knit tie, and my rubber-soled street brogans. Jon's card was in the top drawer of my desk. I sat down there and made a couple of phone calls. Then I folded a pair of swimming trunks inside a zippered plastic bag with my goggles, tucked it in my soft Il Bisonte briefcase, and returned to the kitchen, where I gave my bride a smooch on the lips and Phoebe a peck on the forehead. "Have a good day, or at least try. I'll check in with you when I can. We're going to get through this. Scout's honor."

I went into the vestibule and put on my wool-lined trench coat and gray fedora, which I'd had freshly blocked at Worth & Worth on Fifth Avenue a week ago. Then I hooked Lulu's leash to her collar. "Keep close to me, okay? It's a bit of a riot scene out there."

Merilee joined us in the vestibule and gave me a boa constrictor hug. "Darling, you're not going to get yourself all tangled up in this, are you?" she asked me, her brow furrowing with concern.

"Trust me, there is absolutely no chance of that happening."

CHAPTER SIX

Needless to say, but I'll say it anyway, Michael Jackson's insipid "Thriller" was blasting away in the coffee shop on Third Avenue and Sixty-Sixth Street, where I met Siena Bing. Since the town house was a crime scene, I couldn't meet her there, and her realty office said she'd be working at home today. Still, she'd sounded pleased to hear my voice on the phone and eager to meet.

Siena was drinking tea and sucking on a cough drop. I'm no doctor—I don't even play one on television—but she looked extremely unwell to me. She was pale, with dark circles under her eyes. Her expensively coiffed hair was pulled back in a rather limp ponytail. Her shoulders sagged inside the bulky, shapeless cardigan she was wearing. She was by no means dressed to show anyone a multimillion-dollar home today.

I ordered coffee as Lulu circled around three times under the table and curled up on my feet.

"I was surprised to hear from you, Hoagy," Siena said, sipping her tea as my coffee arrived. "I came up with two possible explanations. One is that you want to surprise your new bride by buying her the Singleton house as a wedding present. The other is that you're hitting on me."

"I'm absolutely not hitting on you. I just got married yesterday, remember?"

"As if that slows you guys down," she said, rolling her eyes.

"Which guys?"

"Rich, good-looking ones who are accustomed to getting whatever and whomever they want."

"You seem to have a rather low opinion of me."

"I'm accustomed to showing houses to wealthy married men, and they invariably seem to think that I go along with the package. If I'm wrong about you, I apologize."

"Apology accepted. Have you spoken to Lieutenant Golden today?"

"No, I haven't. I'm supposed to steer clear of the Singleton house, so I'm working at home this morning and trying to chase this flu bug."

"He hasn't phoned you?"

"Why would he phone me?"

"I have what may be some alarming news for you. If I'm way off base, then it's my turn to apologize, but I thought you ought to know that the medical examiner's autopsy revealed Junior was HIV positive. He had the AIDS virus."

Siena's eyes widened before she took a sip of her tea and said, "Why are you telling me this?"

"Because you had sex with him, didn't you?"

"What makes you jump to that conclusion?"

"Because I knew Junior. He was relentlessly promiscuous, and you're attractive, shapely. Face it, you're a hot babe for a somewhat older woman."

She glared at me. "I'm thirty-six. That makes me 'a somewhat older woman'?"

"Junior was twenty-eight."

"Then I guess it does. Are you suggesting I don't have the flu?"

"I'm suggesting you make an appointment with your doctor to get a blood test. Flu-like symptoms are a symptom of the AIDS virus. When was it that you had sex with Junior?"

"About three weeks ago. He stopped by the house to pick up some things, and we were alone there together. He came on to me and, well, I sort of let him. For some reason, men take one look at me and think I'm quickie material. Do I broadcast slut to you?"

"No, you seem like an ambitious career woman. But that doesn't mean you aren't interested in a long-term relationship."

"He was a very attractive man, not to mention persuasive. And I hadn't been with anyone in months. Maybe I was a bit of a pushover."

"Was he wearing protection?"

She lowered her eyes before she shook her head. "You've come here to tell me that I'm going to die of AIDS, haven't you?"

"No, but I'd advise you to get a blood test, like I said. Talk to your doctor. Get good information."

"If he did give me the AIDS virus, I suppose that makes me a prime candidate for sticking that steak knife in his eyeball. That's why you asked me if

Lieutenant Golden had called me, isn't it? I had no idea Junior was HIV positive. How would I have known that? He seemed perfectly healthy."

"Some people are asymptomatic, I'm told."

"It's not fair!" Her eyes suddenly teared up. She pulled a tissue from her purse and dabbed at them, sniffling. "I don't want to die."

"That's not going to happen. You have access to the best doctors in the world. But it's not a fair world. I don't have to tell you that."

"No, you don't," she said quietly. "What really pisses me off is that if having sex one time with Junior Singleton ends up killing me, it was the worst sex I've ever had. He was a five-minute man. Also a terrible kisser. Way too much tongue. Yech."

"Phoebe also hinted that he was a rotten lover."

"The man climbed Everest, raced Formula One Ferraris . . . I figured he'd be a champ in the sack. Nay, not so." She looked at me uneasily. "Are you going to tell Lieutenant Golden about this?"

"I won't if you don't want me to."

"I'd rather you didn't. I promise I'll tell him if the blood test turns up HIV positive." She reached across the table and clutched my hand. Hers was cold and clammy. "I'm scared, Hoagy."

"I don't blame you. Do you have people you're close to? Family?"

"I'm an only child. My parents live in Syracuse. I'd swallow a bottle of liquid Drano before I'd move back there. But I'm tight with a couple of girlfriends."

"That's good. And if I can ever help you . . ."

"You could buy that town house."

I grinned at her. "Is your motto 'Waste no opportunity'?"

"I was just kidding."

"No, you weren't."

"Okay, you're right. But I know you'll never buy it. You could never be happy there. It's haunted."

"I'm afraid so."

She signaled our waitress for the check. "Thank you for reaching out to me. I appreciate your concern, although it puzzles me. You're an incredibly successful young author who's married to a movie star. You barely know me, yet you've taken the time to be so nice to me. What's your agenda?"

"Haven't got one."

Siena Bing let out a mocking laugh, which she paid for with a deep, rumbling cough. "Don't shit a shitter," she responded, a hard-nosed Manhattan real estate broker to the bone. "Everyone has an agenda."

◆

Ten o'clock in the morning was a good time to swim my laps in the pool at the Racquet and Tennis Club. I was usually the only one who was using the pool then, which was a good thing because it meant my vigilant lifeguard, who ran alongside the pool next to me barking her head off, lap after lap, didn't annoy anyone. What made Lulu's self-appointed mission truly ironic was that she was the only dog I'd ever met who didn't know how to swim. The first time she joined me there for my hydrotherapy, she ambled into the pool and sank straight to the bottom, glug-glug-glug. I had to pull her out, sputtering and gaacking. I tried to teach her to dog paddle, which I'd thought was a canine instinct, but Lulu was no normal canine. At least she never made the mistake of going into the water again. Just stayed safely alongside me to make sure I was okay.

After I took a quick shower and toweled off, exhausted but pleased by how the strength was returning to my trapezius, I dressed, stowed my wet trunks inside their plastic zipper bag in my briefcase, and checked my phone machine from one of the phones in the lobby.

To my surprise, I had a message from Phoebe's mother, Pippa: "Hoagy, I want you to write a major cover story on Junior for SHE. I've already spoken to your agent, Alberta, and we've negotiated a nice, fat fee. Please swing by the office today so we can talk. Call me when you can. The sooner the better."

I glanced at Grandfather's Benrus. It was a quarter past 11. I had arranged an eleven thirty appointment with Junior's British friend Jon Porterfield that was a two-minute walk away. I phoned Pippa and was put through to her immediately.

"Hoagy!" she brayed in my ear. "Good of you to get back to me."

"Good of you to call me. I'm intrigued, naturally."

"How soon can you swing by?"

"Would twelve thirty work for you?"

"Perfect. I'll have my assistant arrange for lunch to be brought in."

◆

The New York City office of Jon's international investment firm was located almost directly across Park Avenue from the Racquet and Tennis Club on the twentieth floor of Lever House, the landmark

1952 rectangular office building built in what was known as the International Style, which meant that it had said goodbye to ornamentation in favor of unadorned steel and glass. Lever House had a lot to answer for, in my humble opinion, because it created the template for the countless soul-free shoebox office buildings that took over Midtown Manhattan in the years to come.

I hooked Lulu's leash on, and we strolled out into the blustery winter air, my fedora parked firmly on my head, crossed Park, entered the lobby of Lever House, and caught an elevator to the twentieth floor, where I gave the male receptionist my name. Jon's firm was one of the top boutique investment houses in the world that catered to the super-rich. It had offices not only in New York and London but also in Geneva, Tokyo, and Singapore. The firm owned a one-bedroom co-op in a doorman building on West Fifty-Ninth with a view of Central Park that was available for Jon's use whenever he was in New York.

The receptionist was a tall, slim young man wearing a black suit. When I gave him my name, he buzzed Jon, who came out promptly to greet me and to ask him to hold his calls. Jon was in his early thirties and dressed expensively and well—a bespoke

Savile Row charcoal double-breasted suit that artfully contoured his body, a sparkling white shirt, and a blue-and-cream striped silk tie. He was about five feet eight and structured on the borderline somewhere between chubby and tubby. Let me put it this way—Jon Porterfield was not someone I would ever want to see naked in the sauna. All I could picture was billowing rolls of pink blubber. Handsome the man was not. He was toothy, jowly, and prematurely bald. When I'd met him before, he'd struck me as someone who had every reason to be proud of his professional accomplishments. Yet his humor was tinged with low self-esteem despite how rich and successful he was. Possibly, he'd been picked on back when he was a fat schoolkid, like Piggy in *Lord of the Flies.* He was an ideal friend for Junior—not exactly a flunky but definitely someone who was thrilled to bask in Junior's glow and procure anything or anyone that Junior's heart desired. The Junior Singletons of the world always seemed to have a Jon Porterfield in their orbit.

He patted Lulu on the head and mustered a sad smile as we started down the corridor to his office, which was small and sparsely furnished. No personal adornments at all. Just a stack of files on the desk, a yellow legal notepad, and three phones. I suspected he shared the space with the firm's other international brokers when they found themselves in New York for a few days or weeks. His own office in London was no doubt far grander.

"I'm glad you rang me up, Hoagy. I'd hoped you would. Have a seat." He closed the door, took off his suit jacket, put it on a wooden hanger, and hung it on a hook on the back of the door, which was a mistake. Not the hanging-it-on-the-back-of-the-door part. The taking-his-jacket-off part. He had significant, broth-scented sweat stains under his armpits in what was not a particularly warm office. I wondered if anticipating my arrival had made him nervous. And if so, why? He settled himself in the black leather chair behind his desk.

"I met Junior when we were freshmen," I said as I sat across the desk from him. Lulu curled up under my chair with a yawn. She gets quite a workout pulling lifeguard duty. "I always liked the guy. He was so alive. I keep hoping I'll get the image of that steak knife in his eyeball out of my head, but I can't."

"Give it time. It'll go away. I wish the two of us could toast him with a brandy and soda, but alcohol is now strictly verboten during business hours in the New York office. I'm told the era of the two-martini lunch is over on this side of the pond. It's considered a sign of weakness. One is supposed to go to a gym and pump iron instead, and subsist on Perrier water. In London, we still enjoy a drink before lunch, but we've always been much more civilized." Jon folded his soft, pink hands on the desk before him. They immediately began to tremble, so he lowered them into his lap. "Now then, how may I be of help?"

"Jon, I received some very disturbing news this morning from the police lieutenant who's investigating Junior's murder."

"I can't imagine something more disturbing than the aforementioned image of finding an old friend lying on his dressing room floor with a steak knife in his eyeball. But do go on, please."

"The medical examiner and his team were up all night performing an autopsy. It seems that Junior was HIV positive. He had the AIDS virus."

Jon's eyes widened in shock. "You're joking."

"I'm afraid not. The lieutenant asked me if I had any idea whom he might have picked it up from. I didn't. I don't. Do you?"

He stiffened. "What makes you think I'd know?"

"I didn't mean to offend you. It's just that he and I didn't roister together like you two did."

"We did most of that in London or my country place in Devon, while Phoebe was home alone here," he admitted. "Wild parties that would go on for days. Drug-fueled orgies is what they were. Word would get out, and fifty people would show up. I only knew about half of them." He paused, shaking his head. "I never did understand why he married Phoebe. She's certainly a decorative girl, nice manners and so forth. But, God, she's dull."

"A wild child she's not," I agreed. "Did Junior ever play for both teams?"

He frowned at me. "Sorry?"

"Did he have sex with male partners?"

"Aah . . ." Jon pursed his lips primly. "He'd let a bloke suck his cock if there was a flesh pile, but he never took it up the pooper, or vice versa. He wasn't gay. I can say that with some degree of certainty."

"You mentioned drugs. Did he ever shoot heroin?"

"He did."

"As recently as in the past month or two?"

"I can't say for certain, but it's possible."

"Did you ever share a needle with him?"

"No. Not with him or anyone else. Needles scare the piss out of me. Snorting coke is my vice of choice."

"Would you happen to know anything about his sex life here in New York? Any idea who he'd been seeing lately?"

He frowned. "I know he was seeing someone for a while, but he broke it off because she kept making demands of him. Wanted exclusive rights, as it were. Junior liked his freedom, and if he saw a girl he wanted, he considered it his God-given right to have her. I can personally attest to that. There was one in London last year, Cynthia, whom I'd been shagging for a couple of months," he recalled. "More than shagging, actually. I was pretty serious about her. And it was mutual, to my way of seeing things. She invited me to dinner with her parents. Nice girl. Smart. An architect. Anyway, when Junior stopped off in London for a week on his way to the Alps to ski, I threw a dinner party for him at my flat. Maybe a dozen people or so, and I realized the two of them had disappeared before the dessert was served. Walked in on him fucking her in my bed. When she saw me standing there, utterly crushed, she gasped and said, 'I can explain, Jon.' I said, 'Don't bother,' and left the room. It broke my heart, Hoagy. She called me three or four times that week. Said she'd been drunk, that things got out of hand, and that she was so, so sorry. Begged me to forgive her. Swore it didn't change how she felt about me. But it sure as hell changed how I felt about her. And that was the end of that."

"Did Junior call her again?"

"What for? She was just a piece of ass he fucked at a party. I doubt he even knew her name."

"You must have been furious with him."

"I couldn't be. Junior was who he was. I always made special allowances for him. After all, there are only a tiny handful of genuinely special men like Junior in the whole world at any one time."

I nodded, appalled that Jon wouldn't forgive his apologetic girlfriend but didn't blame his unapologetic male friend. Unless, that is, he was lying to me. Unless he never forgave Junior for having his way with Cynthia, and when the opportunity arose, stuck that steak knife in Junior's eyeball as payback.

But why would he have taken two knives?

He gazed out his office window at the lunch hour traffic on Park Avenue, twenty stories below. "Poor Junior. I'm going to miss him."

"You mentioned he'd broken it off with the woman he'd been seeing here lately," I said. "Was there anyone new in his life?"

"As a matter of fact, there was. Last time I saw him, which was the weekend before last, he mentioned he was getting it on with a former idol of his. He was quite into her, actually."

I leaned forward slightly. "And who might this former idol be?"

"She used to be the lead singer of a punk rock band that had a hit song a few years back. Please don't ask me the name of the song. I wasn't a punk fan."

"I was. Used to spend a lot of time at the clubs when I first moved to New York. CBGB, Max's Kansas City. I saw the Sex Pistols, Blondie, Buster Poindexter . . . Did he tell you what his former idol's name was?"

"Mona."

"Mona Dale? The Mona Dale from Four Hundred Blows?"

"That's right. I take it her name means something to you."

"I'll say. Mona Dale was a major punk sex symbol. Almost as big as Debbie Harry. She had spiky pink hair, a great bod, wore incredibly tight, slinky clothes, and had the naughtiest voice. So Junior was seeing her?"

"Pretty hot and heavy for the past few weeks."

"How did he meet her?"

"In line at the Department of Motor Vehicles."

"That sounds like a meet-cute if ever I heard one."

"Sounds like a what?"

"A meet-cute. It's a movie expression. I should stop hanging around with a film star. Oh, wait, I can't. I married her yesterday." Lulu let out a small yip, her tail thumping. "I wonder if Mona shoots up?"

"Wouldn't surprise me. That punk crowd did a lot of heroin. Sid Vicious died of an OD, didn't he? It was front-page news in London."

"Had Junior been shooting up lately?"

"I don't know for certain. He may have been. He was partial to slumming, and the two often go together."

"Slumming?"

"He had a bizarre taste for Black streetwalkers, the kind you find working the sidewalks late at night in hot pants, fishnet hose, and go-go boots. He told me there's a supermarket on Broadway up at West Eighty-Sixth Street where they work the sidewalk after closing time, eight or ten of them."

I was quite familiar with that stretch of sidewalk in front of Sloan's supermarket, since it was near the dirt cheap, unheated fifth-floor walk-up on West Ninety-Third I'd called home until Merilee invited me to move in with her three months ago. It was known as Strutters' Walk. I was also well aware that most of the girls were addicts. Possibly Junior had shared a needle with one of them, and that was how he'd picked up the AIDS virus. "How often did Junior pay a visit there?"

"Whenever he got bored or restless. He lived for thrills, you see, and shooting up with a streetwalker was his idea of a thrill. But he wasn't a heroin addict. My God, he couldn't have climbed Mount Everest if he was one, could he?"

CHAPTER SEVEN

The offices of SHE magazine were a short walk away on the sixteenth floor of 485 Madison Avenue between East Fifty-First and Fifty-Second Streets, which also happened to be the same building in which the offices of *MAD* magazine were located. It amused me to no end to think that Pippa Trowbridge, New York's arbiter of style and sophistication, rode the same elevator to work with disheveled satirists like Dave Berg, Al Jaffee, and the great Don Martin, peerless creator of Fester Bestertester and Karbunkle.

SHE office was not like that of any magazine I'd ever visited. It was more like that of a high-end interior decorating firm—elegantly furnished, plushly carpeted, and hushed. The reception desk in the waiting room was French provincial, as were the chairs.

The receptionist, a slim, well-dressed young brunette, had the self-importance of a Yalie or Smithie. When I gave her my name and the purpose of my visit, she said not one word to me in response, just picked up her phone, dialed a number, and spoke to someone in a discreet murmur.

A moment later, another slim, well-dressed young Yalie or Smithie appeared in the doorway and said, "Mr. Hoag? I'm Pippa's personal assistant, Tiffany Tatum."

"Lucky you. This must be quite an exciting place to work."

"Exciting is the word for it. I started out here as a summer intern while I was still at New Haven"—Yalie it was—"and was thrilled when Pippa offered me a full-time position two years ago."

"You've lasted two whole years? You must have some hard bark on you, appearances to the contrary. She is not the easiest person to get along with."

"It's just bluster," Tiffany said mildly. "I tune it out. I learned how from my father, whose normal speaking voice is a roar. I'm a huge admirer of your work, by the way. Not to mention your taste in women and basset hounds."

"Thank you, Tiffany. Say hello to Lulu."

She bent down and petted her. "Hi there, sweetie."

"Were you acquainted with Junior?"

She reddened. "Why would you ask me that?"

"Because Pippa's daughter, Phoebe, was married to him. I thought your paths might have crossed."

"No, they never did," she said as she led me down a corridor of offices. The faint scent of an alluring perfume wafted behind her.

"I like your perfume. What is it?"

"It's called L'Interdit. Givenchy created it for Audrey Hepburn."

"I suppose if you're going to smell like someone, Audrey Hepburn isn't a bad choice. Better her than Sly Stallone."

She responded with a girlish giggle.

As we strode past one office after another, I noticed Pippa only employed those who were slim, attractive, confident, smartly attired, and unburdened by moles, blackheads, whiteheads, or warts. I had no doubt that Pippa personally inspected each of them from head to toe for SHE suitability. No men worked there, seemingly. Therefore, not surprisingly, I was noticed as I was led to Pippa's office at the end of the hall. I was, after all, a famous, dashingly attired author who was accompanied by the most adorable thirty-two-pound sidekick in New York City.

"I hope to write a novel myself someday," Tiffany said. "Have any advice?"

"There's nothing to it. Just sit in a room by yourself banging your head against the wall for four years and presto, you'll be on the cover of *Time*."

She giggled girlishly again as we arrived at the open door of Pippa's office, which resembled that of a senior partner in a white-shoe law firm aside from the half-dozen easels surrounding her desk that displayed blown-up photos of everything from cover art to Tuscan villas to the latest in spring rain jackets.

Pippa was on the phone barking out words. "I'm thinking spring. The four springiest places to go, what to do when you get there, and with whom to do it . . . Shut up, I'm still talking . . . I'm thinking daffodils, green grass, pedicures . . . Still talking! I'm thinking about the four hottest young male actors we should be drooling over. Start running with that and get back to me by the end of the day."

She hung up without saying goodbye, reached across the desk, and forcefully shook my hand. "Thank you for coming by on such short notice, Stewart. I know this is a grim day for you, but for me, work is always the best medicine. Please, have a seat."

I had a seat. Pippa was dressed in black. I don't know if it was out of mourning for Junior or if she'd simply chosen to wear black that day. A pair of reading glasses was nestled in her frosted blond hair. I found myself staring at that unlined, unreal Dr. Lookgood face of hers. I found it creepy, as if she were wearing a mask made of human flesh.

"How is my Phoebe doing?"

"She's coping." I didn't know whether Pippa was aware of the medical examiner's report that Junior was HIV positive, so I kept quiet about it. "Being with Merilee is good for her. She helps Phoebe keep her spirits up."

"Does Lieutenant Golden have any idea yet who did this horrible thing?"

"Not that I'm aware of."

Lulu waddled over to her side of the desk and was immediately entranced by the scent of Pippa's hands. Kept nosing at her fingers and licking them.

"Lulu seems to like your hand cream."

Pippa smiled faintly. "I'm not surprised. It's a new product from a company called L'Occitane that comes from Provence. It's all native lavender, oils, and shea butter. I have it on special order because it's not available here yet. Does she go everywhere with you?"

"Lulu has become very attached to me. She's my protector."

Pippa gazed down her nose at me. "She's rather small to serve as a protector, isn't she?"

"She makes up for her lack of size with brains and guile."

Pippa let out a shrill laugh. "You are a hoot, Stewart. I never know when you're teasing me." Then she let out a sigh, abruptly turning serious. "I'm told by a friend at the *Times* that Junior left instructions in his will that if a fatal accident ever befell him, he wished to be buried in the Singleton family plot in the Locust Valley cemetery. Pending release of his body, of course. He is still, I imagine, undergoing autopsy procedures."

"I wouldn't know."

"Does that mean you haven't been in contact with the scrumptious Lieutenant Golden?"

"I'm sorry, did you just call him scrumptious?"

"Laugh all you want . . ."

"I'm not laughing."

"But I'm a lonely woman, Stewart. Age-appropriate men aren't interested in the likes of me. They want someone Phoebe's age."

"I'm sorry to tell you that he isn't available."

"Nonsense. Everyone is available. But enough about him. I was surprised to see you and Merilee with Phoebe at her town house yesterday."

"She wanted me to check it out before we left on our honeymoon. Said that Siena is a real closer and that it would be gone by the time we got back. We're looking for a place, and she'd love for us to buy it."

"Are you interested?"

"Not now, we're not. Actually, I was surprised to see you there."

"Siena's fluffing skills aren't up to my standards. Those paintings in the living room are abysmal. I also think the place needs to be sparkling clean. Phoebe's maid, Katie, should be coming every day, not three times a week. I told Siena she should do something about that."

Lulu, who'd had her fill of Pippa's hand cream, moved over to the doorway and stretched out. The pretty young staffers who caught sight of her there squealed with delight and bent over with perfect posture to pet her and tug at her ears. Lulu loved it.

Pippa did not. "Okay, everyone, this is not a petting zoo! Scoot!" They vanished instantly. "May I be candid with you, Stewart?"

"By all means."

"It didn't surprise me that Phoebe and Junior split up. What surprised me was that he married her in the first place. Mind you, it was a wonderful match for her. He was a handsome, daredevil multimillionaire. The top catch to be had. But I never understood what he saw in her."

"Maybe he was in love with her."

"The Junior Singletons of the world don't fall in love."

"In that case, possibly he saw what I see—a beautiful, intelligent, gentle young woman who could bring some peace into his life."

"Nonsense. Phoebe's my daughter, so I'm allowed to say this—she's a mouse whose idea of a good time is reading poetry and playing the violin. They had nothing in common. I knew it wouldn't last. What I'll never understand is why she didn't hold out for a more generous settlement."

"She'll make out fine. A million in cash plus the sale of the town house. She'll end up with a very nice apartment, a country cottage, and a sizable investment nest egg. Besides, she's still young and lovely. She'll remarry."

Pippa tilted her head at me. "You almost sound as if you're interested in her yourself."

"Nope. There's only one woman in the world for me."

"And what a prize that niece of mine is. I forget, did I put you on our cover when your book became a huge bestseller?"

"*Time* did. *GQ* did. You did not."

"Too late now. Besides, that's not why you're here."

"Why am I here?"

Before she could respond, Tiffany gently nudged Lulu out of the doorway and rolled our lunch cart in.

"I hope you don't mind," Pippa said, "but I never eat a heavy lunch. It makes me sluggish."

"Not at all. This looks just right."

This being a platter of a dozen or so assorted finger sandwiches on white bread with the crusts cut off.

There was roast chicken breast, ham, and egg salad. There were carrot sticks, sliced pears, and apples, and a pot of tea.

Tiffany handed each of us a plate and a cloth napkin and poured the tea. Then she smiled at me as she left us to help ourselves.

Pippa stepped into her private bathroom to wash Lulu's slobber from her fingers before she sat back down and reached for a chicken sandwich. "Where were we?"

"I was waiting for you to tell me what you want me to write for you," I said as I bit into an egg salad sandwich.

"Ah, yes. I consider Junior a symbol of a bygone era of daredevil gentleman adventurers who'd do things like fly biplanes and go hunting for big game in deepest, darkest Africa. You understood what made him tick. The two of you were friends, weren't you?"

"We were classmates. We weren't close friends."

"Have you spoken to any of his close friends?"

"His British chum, Jon Porterfield. He's an international investment broker who may have been his best friend, if Junior had a best friend. Jon seems to think Junior started seeing someone new recently, and that it was hot and heavy."

Pippa nibbled some more on her sandwich, pausing to sip her tea. "Any idea who the young lady is?"

Pippa Longworth was famously nosy and vindictive. With one phone call to Page Six of the *New York Post*, she could destroy anyone if she was so inclined. Consequently, I said, "I have no idea. And very few insights into Junior. He was something of an enigma. I don't have the slightest idea what made him tick."

"Yet you attended Harvard together. Belonged to the same clubs, knew the same people. Furthermore, you're a dashing literary star whose movie star wife is the cousin of Junior's ex-wife. Face it, you're the perfect choice to write a cover profile of him. An appreciation, if you will. Who better than you? You can talk to his friends, collect some colorful anecdotes."

I sipped my tea. "I could, I suppose . . ."

She studied me curiously. "You don't exactly sound enthusiastic. I've made Alberta a very generous offer. But I'm prepared to raise it, if that's what's holding you back."

"Money isn't the issue. I just need some time to mull it over. Junior was an extreme risk-taker. It's been my experience that such people have a darker side to them. I want to try to get a handle on what

Junior's was. I also want to wait until we find out who stuck that steak knife in his eyeball, and why. It seems to me that until Lieutenant Golden figures out who murdered him that I won't really have the hook for any sort of worthwhile profile."

"You're absolutely right, Stewart. I'm stampeding you into this assignment, and I don't mean to. I apologize. It's just that I have a personal stake in it. He was my former son-in-law. Besides, you're not the sort of writer I usually hire for SHE. You're a deep thinker."

Lulu started coughing.

Pippa eyed her with concern. "Why is she doing that?"

"Because she doesn't know how to laugh."

"Take as much time as you need, Stewart. There's no ticking clock. If you wish to be left alone, I'll leave you alone. If you wish to bounce ideas off me, stop by the office any day after six o'clock. We can kick off our shoes, have a glass of wine, and brainstorm it. Believe me, I want the same thing that you want—to understand Junior. Do we have a deal?"

"We have a deal." I deposited my napkin on the lunch cart and stood up. "Thanks for lunch."

"My pleasure." Pippa's eyes gleamed at me. "I still can't believe we didn't put you on our cover."

"Nor can I," I said. "But there's no accounting for taste."

◆

If you needed to locate someone in those days and happened to be in Midtown Manhattan, your best bet was to try the telephone directory center in the main concourse of Grand Central Terminal. It was a fifteen-by-twenty-foot glass-enclosed space that held not only the fat phone books for all five boroughs of New York City but also for most of the major cities in the United States.

I figured I'd start with Manhattan before I worked my way to the outer boroughs. There were four Mona Dales listed in the Manhattan phone book. Two of them lived on Park Avenue, which I figured was a long shot for a former punk singer, unless she's really cleaned up her act. One lived on Duane Street in trendy Tribeca and the other on West Forty-Fifth Street between Eleventh and Twelfth Avenue in Hell's Kitchen, a notoriously crime-ridden, run-down neighborhood that had yet to become even remotely trendy. I jotted down both of those phone numbers and addresses and headed for one of the many pay phones outside of the glass enclosure. Then I fished a dime from my pants pocket and looked down at Lulu. Lulu was looking back up at me with a blank expression. She offered no sage guidance on which Mona I should try first. Don't laugh, you'd be surprised how many times she knows such things.

I opted for the Mona Dale who lived in Tribeca, which was a mistake. She turned out to be a grouchy old woman who was sick of punk rock fans calling her up and wanting to talk to her about her glory days. So next I tried the Hell's Kitchen Mona Dale. Her number was busy. Before I tried it again, I phoned home. Merilee let her machine take it. When she heard me leaving a message, she picked up.

"Hi, darling. What have you been up to?"

"I got in a good swim with my lifeguard, then had a chat with Junior's British friend, Jon Porterfield, per Lieutenant Golden's request."

"Was it productive?"

"Too soon to tell."

"Hoagy, did you or did you not swear to me you weren't going to get mixed up in this?"

"I'm not. Mixed up in it, that is. He just asked me to do him a favor."

"That, dear sir, sounds like an immense load of piffle, if you don't mind my saying so."

"I don't mind a bit. And then after that, and please do not repeat this to a certain blond houseguest, I spent a fun-filled lunch hour with Pippa, who wants me to write a cover story about Junior for SHE. Pippa considered him the symbol of a bygone era of gentleman adventurers and thinks I'd be the perfect candidate to write about him."

"Are you interested?"

"Intrigued, but I told her I won't commit until Lieutenant Golden figures out who killed him. She's willing to wait, so it's on hold for now. Has Phoebe gotten the results of her blood test?"

"Not yet. But the police medical technician hopes to have them by the end of the day."

"And what are you two crazy kids up to now?"

"We're about to get a police escort through the tabloid horde and a ride in a squad car to Meredith's apartment again so Phoebe can pick up the rest of her clothes, her violin, music stand, and whatever else she has there. Somehow, the tabloid lemmings found out that she'd been staying with Meredith. Some idiot in the office at Brearley must have told them. So they're camped out on the sidewalk outside of Meredith's building. Meredith's not happy about it and has very politely asked Phoebe to move out. We'll bring her things here until she can find a place. It's not a huge load. The patrolmen will help us tote it inside."

"Have I told you today that I love you?"

"You have never told me that."

"Have so."

"Have not."

"Have so."

"Have not."

"Well, I do. Love you, that is."

"And it's a damned good thing, too."

"Because . . . ?"

"Because I love you, too, mister."

After we hung up, I tried the Hell's Kitchen Mona Dale again, wondering if I'd get another busy signal. Possibly, she had the phone off the hook.

She didn't. It rang. She picked it up and said, "Hello?" Her voice sounded hoarse and raspy.

"Mona? My name is Stewart Hoag. I was a friend of Junior's."

After a long silence, she said, "So . . . ?"

"I was wondering if I could stop by and talk to you about him for a few minutes."

"What for?"

"I'm the one who found his body with that knife stuck in his eyeball. I can't shake the horror of seeing him that way. I'm just . . . really upset."

"Not as upset as I am, trust me. I had to call in sick today."

"Are you sick?"

"No, I feel fine, aside from the part where I can't stop crying. Fuck it, come on over. It's Six-Eighteen West Forty-Fifth. Hell's Kitchen, baby. Ring the buzzer for B, as in basement."

"Thanks, I appreciate it. I'll see you in a little while."

"Wait, what did you say your name was?"

"Stewart Hoag. Most people call me Hoagy."

"Could you bring me a six-pack of Pabst Blue Ribbon?"

"Be happy to."

I was starting toward the Vanderbilt entrance to Grand Central when the hairs on the back of my neck stood up and my pulse quickened. That's what happens to me when I get the spooks, by which I mean an instinct telling me that someone is tailing me. It's a survival instinct that comes from the years I spent walking home alone late at night on West Ninety-Third Street, which qualifies as a borderline ghetto. I'd been mugged twice in the four years I'd lived there. Both times, I'd had that same instinct just before it happened.

I stopped and looked around, scanning the mob of people crisscrossing the terminal. I saw no one paying any special attention to me. At my feet, Lulu looked up at me in curiosity, wondering why I'd stopped. Bassets have world-class scent skills, second only to bloodhounds, yet she seemingly smelled no one with whom we'd been in recent contact, such as Jon, with his brothy, sweat-stained armpits, or Tiffany and her Audrey Hepburn perfume, or Pippa and her precious lavender-scented hand cream. I asked myself why one of them would be tailing me. Why would anyone? Was it my imagination? Had to be, because just as quickly as the spooks had hit me, they were gone.

We resumed walking and caught a cab on Vanderbilt. I gave the cabbie Mona's address. As he worked his way west across Midtown on Forty-Second Street, I did find myself turning around to see if someone in a cab was tailing us. What can I tell you? Paranoia runs deep. Into your heart it will creep. But no one seemed to be. Lulu, who still didn't seem the least bit bothered, calmly stretched out on the seat beside me and dozed.

When I spotted a bodega on the corner of West Forty-Fourth Street and Eleventh Avenue, I asked the cabbie to drop us there. Went in and bought a cold six-pack of Pabst. We walked up to West Forty-Fifth and started our way toward Mona's building at #618 when I suddenly felt the spooks again, my pulse quickening. And this time I wasn't alone. Lulu raised her nose in the air and let out a low whoop. Now that we were no longer in crowded Grand Central, surrounded by hundreds of different perfumes, colognes, hair tonics, and deodorants, not to mention Zaro's Bakery and the Oyster Bar, she'd gotten a definite familiar whiff. I turned around and scanned the street, which consisted mostly of tenements, complete with fire escapes. There was also a warehouse where burly guys were unloading crates from the back of a truck. I saw no cab idling with someone slumped low in the back seat. No one lingering in the shadows on the sidewalk across the street.

But it wasn't my imagination. Lulu was on alert now as we approached the building—right up until I rang the buzzer for B as in basement and Mona buzzed us in. Then she relaxed. I didn't. I kept wondering who was tailing me, and why.

Mona's building was neither the nicest nor the most run-down on the block. It was just a dump in a state of non-genteel decay. The entry hall smelled as if someone had given the floor a thorough scrubbing with Pine-Sol as recently as 1967. We went down a dimly lit stairway to a steel door. I knocked on it and said who I was, and the one-time punk idol let me in, reaching for the Pabst as she yanked me inside.

There were no windows in her damp basement apartment, which was a one-room studio with a bare cement floor and a flickering fluorescent ceiling fixture for lighting. Mona had a bed, unmade, an aged Naugahyde easy chair that looked as if she'd dragged it in off the street, and a color TV that was tuned to a soap opera with the sound turned off. There was no kitchen to speak of. Just a hot plate, microwave, and mini fridge. No sink. There was a sink in the bathroom, which dripped. The toilet made burbling noises. There was no shower or bathtub. The prevailing odor of a dead mouse indicated a mouse had died somewhere in the apartment recently. Lulu stayed by the door, grunting sourly. She hates mice, dead or alive.

It was a far cry from the multimillion-dollar East Side town house that Junior had once shared with

Phoebe. And Mona was a far cry from the lovely, genteel Phoebe. She was four years older than the last time I'd seen her perform at CBGB, but she was still plenty sexy in a slinky, sleazy sort of way. She wore a torn skintight sleeveless black T-shirt with nothing underneath it, which afforded me a view of the side cleavage of her generously sized boobs. Also of her armpits, which she didn't shave. Or bother to take soap and water to with any great regularity. The odor emanating from them was fighting it out with that of her bare feet, which were exceptionally dirty. She painted her toenails black, unless it was just accumulated grime. I truly didn't feel like looking too closely. She no longer wore her hair spiky and pink. She'd now opted for a 1950s boys' crew cut that she'd dyed a color remarkably similar to Tang.

Her eyes were red from crying.

She lit an unfiltered Lucky Strike and dragged deeply on it. Took an opener to a can of Pabst and popped it open. Didn't offer me one or invite me to sit down. Just took a long gulp and put the remaining five cans in her mini fridge, which was empty except for a takeout Chinese food container.

"I was a huge fan," I said. "Saw Four Hundred Blows perform at least a dozen times. You mesmerized me. I couldn't take my eyes off of you."

She looked me up and down doubtfully. "You were a punk fan?"

"Still am. Don't let my bespoke tailoring fool you. I've got a Sex Pistols T-shirt on under this dress shirt."

Mona peered at Lulu. "How come your dog is huddled by the door that way?"

"She's afraid of mice."

"Then she wouldn't be happy living here."

"Tell me, what happened to Four Hundred Blows?"

She shrugged. "What always happens to bands. Egos get in the way. I was fucking Spanky, our lead guitarist, if you can call what he played lead guitar, and when I started fucking our drummer, Miguel, too, they had a major falling out and everything just fell apart. We had one song, "Roadkill," that made the charts, but we were so stoned all the time that we didn't have any other songs to record. We were strictly about chaos. We'd go out on stage with no idea what we were going to play. The band would jam super loud, and I'd scream whatever lyrics came into my head. We didn't make music. We made noise.

Our record company dropped us, and our manager said bye-bye, too, and that was the end of it. I did try to launch a solo career, since I was kind of sexy in those days."

"You're still plenty sexy."

Mona treated me to a crooked smile. "But that went nowhere. The music business is incredibly cruel. It destroys people. It almost destroyed me. I shot smack for two years after that."

"Do you still shoot it?"

"No, I'm clean now. Have to be. They drug test us at work. If I show up with so much as a trace of pot in my pee, I'll get fired. My biggest vice now is grape lollipops."

Which explained the bag of them the forensics team had found in the pocket of Junior's duffel coat.

"He was supposed to come see me last night," she said, her voice cracking and her eyes tearing up. "I-I wondered why he stood me up. He never, ever did that before. When I saw what happened to him on the news this morning, I couldn't stop crying, so I called in sick."

"Where do you work?"

"The Department of Motor Vehicles on West Thirty-First Street."

"You're kidding."

"Pretty funny, isn't it? A sneering punk rocker working behind the counter of the DMV. But it's weirdly perfect. People expect to be treated like shit there, and I'm damned good at it."

"How did you end up working there?"

"I took a civil service exam after I got clean. It was either that or wait tables in a dive bar. I'm smarter than I look. I aced the exam, and they assigned me there. That's how I met Junior. When he came in to renew his driver's license, he stood there staring at me and said, 'You're Mona Dale. I used to be madly in love with you.' I said, 'You look weirdly familiar yourself, handsome. Have I seen your picture in the paper?' And he said, 'Probably. I do crazy things like climb to the top of Mount Everest and race Ferraris in the European Grand Prix.' His application said his name was Claude Singleton Junior. I said, 'Sure, you're Junior Singleton. You're not only famous and great-looking, but you're worth hundreds of millions.' "

"And what did he say?"

"He said, 'I didn't actually do anything to earn it. I just inherited it.' Almost like he felt guilty about it or something. I said, 'Listen, I get off at five. Buy a six-pack of Pabst and wait outside for me. I'll take you home and fuck you like no one's ever fucked you before.' At five, he was standing outside with a sixer of Pabst, looking as delicious as a man can look. He hailed a cab. As soon as we got in and he closed the door, I stuck my tongue down his throat, and his hands were under my blouse, squeezing my nipples. By the time the cab got here, we'd practically undressed each other. We were so hot for each other it was unbelievable. It was one of those instant chemistry things. We were naked by the time we made it down the stairs to my door. Somehow, I managed to unlock it, and we fucked our brains out all night. He was the best fuck I've ever had, and I've had my share, believe me."

"Oh, I do," I said, thinking her rating of Junior's prowess was a far cry from what I'd heard from Phoebe and Siena.

She stubbed out her Lucky and lit another one.

"You smoke a lot."

"Want one?"

"No, thanks. I quit. You don't see many people smoking Luckys anymore. LSMFT."

She peered at me, mystified. "Say what?"

"LSMFT. 'Lucky Strike Means Fine Tobacco.' Don't you remember their slogan from the old TV commercials?"

"We didn't have a TV," she said in a flat voice. "Me and my mom lived in a cold water flat in Hoboken. Bathtub in the kitchen, toilet down the hall."

"What about your dad?"

"What dad? Mom got knocked up when she was in high school, ran away from home, and never saw him again. Raised me by herself. Paid the rent by hooking. When I was sixteen, I ran away myself and headed here in search of fame and fortune. All I found out was what it was like to be starved and homeless. I was crashing in an abandoned building in the South Bronx when I met Spanky, who played the guitar in the subway for quarters, and we decided to form a band. We called it Four Hundred Blows because that was the title of his favorite foreign film. It didn't have anything to do with blow jobs, which was what our fans always thought."

I nodded. "The Four Hundred Blows was Truffaut's first film."

"I wouldn't know about that. Never saw it. Like I said, we had one hit song and a club following, but when it came to money, it was strictly pass the hat.

Usually, there were four or five of us living together in places like this. Actually, worse than this. At least I have a bathroom here."

I glanced around, Lulu grunting at me sourly again. "You have a civil service job. You could afford something a lot nicer than this."

Mona stubbed out her Lucky and lit another one. "That's not who I am. This is the only way I know how to live."

"How is your health?"

"My health? Why are you asking?"

"Because the medical examiner discovered that Junior was HIV positive."

Her eyes widened. "How'd you hear that?"

"My wife's cousin was married to him."

"You mean Fee-bee?" she asked, her voice filled with disdain.

"That's right."

"She was all over the news on TV this morning. She's Merilee Nash's cousin."

"Yes, I know."

"You're married to a movie star?" she asked, notably unimpressed.

"That's right."

"Are you an actor, too? You're certainly good-looking enough."

"No, I'm a writer."

"Well, Fee-bee has no need to worry. Junior hadn't gone near her in months. He got everything he could handle from me, four or five nights a week. He was so horny for me we'd fuck our brains out until dawn. I'd have to call in sick. God, we were crazy about each other." Her eyes teared up. She swiped at them with the back of her hand and drained her Pabst.

"I find this interesting."

"You find what interesting?"

"I've spoken to other women who found him profoundly unsatisfying as a sexual partner."

"That's because they weren't what he wanted."

"And what was it that he wanted?"

"Pure, unadulterated white trash. He loved the way I smell. He loved this shithole of an apartment. We'd eat Chinese takeout and watch crappy TV shows. Never went out to a restaurant or a movie or anything. We always stayed here."

"I realize this is personal, but did he wear a condom?"

"Always." She fetched another can of Pabst from her mini fridge, opened it, and drank deeply. "And

I do mean always. Back when I sang in the clubs, I picked up every kind of sexually transmitted disease you've ever heard of. I did not want to go down that road again, so I made sure there was a supply here." Mona fell silent for a moment. Reached for another Lucky and lit it. "He told me once that he hated the boredom of life. He had all of this money, but he wasn't happy being who he was, so he was always searching for something. He went all around the world searching. Lately, he found what he was looking for right here with me, an ex-punk rocker who works for the DMV. Don't ask me to explain it, because I can't. I only know it was for real. I mean, think about it. He had a luxury suite at the Sherry-Netherland. We could have stayed there together. Ordered fancy room service. Soaked in a hot tub. But he didn't want that, don't you see? He wanted this. Kept coming back. He always came back. I-I can't believe he won't ever come back again."

"You loved him, didn't you?"

"What the fuck is love? I don't even know what that word means. Besides, he was seeing someone else, too."

"Who?"

"No idea. I just know he was getting sick of her because she was clingy."

"Did it bother you that he had another woman?"

"Sometimes, but I knew that what we had together was real. Besides, you have to let people be who they are."

A mouse skittered across the floor into the bathroom. Lulu let out a whimper. Mona didn't even seem to notice it.

"Did you ever meet any of his friends?"

"No, never."

"Do you have any idea who stuck that knife in his eyeball? Or why?"

Mona shrugged her slinky shoulders. "Fee-bee was divorcing him, but they both seemed pretty cool about the whole thing. I mean, there didn't seem to be bad blood between them. I can't imagine she did it. He said she was a priss."

"A priss?"

"She wouldn't go down on him. They were so totally different that I asked him why he married her. He told me he was feeling depressed and thought that maybe the ultimate adventure would be to try leading a normal life. She was perfect wifey material. Pretty and classy. But within a few months, he knew that he wasn't cut out for normal life. Plus, he didn't love her. He loved me. It's too bad, actually."

"What is, Mona?"

"That I always made him wear a condom. If I hadn't, then he could have given me AIDS. Junior was the only person who ever made me feel alive. So what's the point of living now? I go to the DMV every day and get yelled at by assholes. I may as well be dead, too. I wish I was." She took a last drag on her Lucky and tossed the butt across the cement floor. "I do. I really, really do."

CHAPTER EIGHT

Whoever had tailed us to Mona's apartment didn't seem to be waiting around outside in the blustery winter cold. I felt no spooky vibes. And Lulu didn't let out a low whoop of warning. Mostly, she just seemed happy to be out of Mona's shithole basement. When I glanced at Grandfather's Benrus, I was surprised to discover that more than ninety minutes had disappeared while we'd been in there.

I found a pay phone on Eleventh Avenue, called the number Golden had given me, and left the number of the pay phone I was using.

He returned my call in less than two minutes. "I was wondering when I'd hear from you. Got anything for me?"

"I've definitely picked up information that will be of interest to you."

"Lieutenant Mitry wasn't kidding. Where are you?"

"In Hell's Kitchen."

"What are you doing there?"

"Freezing my ass off talking to you on a pay phone on Eleventh Avenue. Lulu's ears are turning blue."

"When can we meet?"

"Now would be a very good time. I'll meet you anywhere as long as it's not a dreary cop diner."

He let out an annoyed sigh. "Name the place."

"Zut Alors."

"Wait, you just said what?"

"Zut Alors. It's a bistro on West Forty-Fifth in the theater district. I'll see you in twenty minutes. Oh, hey, Lieutenant?"

"What is it, Hoagy?"

"How did you make out today?"

He didn't bother to answer me. Just hung up. I didn't know the man very well, but I took it to mean he wasn't happy.

◆

It was 5:30 when I got there. Golden was standing at the crowded bar in his cocoa-brown double knit suit, bell-bottomed trousers, and platform shoes, drinking a mug of coffee and looking tense. Zut Alors was a theater district hangout. The bar was popular day and night with Broadway critics, gossip columnists, and publicists. The restaurant did a good business with theatergoers before and after the curtain.

"There are plenty of tables right now," I said as Lulu and I approached Golden. "Let's grab one so we can talk."

We sat, and as always, Lulu circled three times before she curled up on my feet. Golden ordered another coffee, and I ordered coffee and a Macallan single malt Scotch to get rid of the chill in my bones. Our waiter poured our coffees right away. I sipped mine gratefully, enjoying that it was hot and strong. When the Scotch arrived a moment later, I sipped it even more gratefully, feeling its warmth all the way down to my toes.

Golden peered across the table at me. "So what have you got for me?"

"Not much for small talk, are you, Lieutenant?"

"I'm trying to catch the Society Slayer. When a murderer gets a tabloid nickname, that means I have zero time for small talk."

"For starters, I met Siena Bing, Phoebe's Realtor, at a coffee shop in the East Sixties."

"Time out. I didn't ask you to talk to her."

"I'm aware of that, but you may have noticed yesterday at the crime scene that she had a nasty cough. You certainly noticed that she's quite attractive. A 'dish,' I believe you called her. Since she and Junior had no doubt been alone in the house together when he stopped by to pick up his things, there was no doubt in my mind that he boinked her. I thought she ought to know that the medical examiner had discovered Junior was HIV positive."

"Understood. And how did she take the news?"

"Not well."

"Meaning she did boink him?"

"Would I be telling you this story if she hadn't? She admitted that they'd had unprotected sex on one occasion. Broke down sobbing. She was very upset. Let's face it, finding out that you may have the AIDS virus is life-altering news." The waiter came by and asked me if I wanted another shot of Macallan. I did.

"I urged her to see her doctor right away and get a blood test. She said she would."

After the waiter returned with my Macallan and topped off Golden's coffee, Golden took a sip and said, "I'm glad you freelanced on me. You're already paying dividends."

"I am? How so?"

"Siena Bing has known that she's HIV positive ever since she got a blood test ten days ago. Her doctor told us he recommends it to all single, sexually active patients who show up at his office with flu-like symptoms."

"I thought doctor-patient information was supposed to be confidential."

Golden shrugged. "We have our ways of getting around that."

"So you're telling me she looked me right in the eye this morning and lied to me. I can't believe she did that. What am I saying? Of course I can. What I can't believe is that I fell for it."

"It happens to the best of us. Let it go. She's a shrewd piece of work. A top performer for a high-end realty agency. If word leaked out that she has the AIDs virus, they'd drop-kick her."

"So does this make her a suspect?"

"I'm planning to question her tomorrow. She's certainly a person of interest. She has keys to the house and one hell of a motive for getting even with Junior. But here's what I want to know: Why would she take that second knife?"

"Good question."

"Thank you," he said dryly. "Who did you talk to after Siena?"

"Jon Porterfield, Junior's friend from London, as you requested. He's a major-league international investment broker who spends a lot of his time here. Despite his buttoned-down job and buttoned-down appearance, Jon's a bit of a wild man who seems to know everything about Junior's sex life, up to and including that he frequented bisexual orgies at Jon's country house."

Golden narrowed his eyes at me. "Junior was bisexual?"

"Jon said that if Junior was stoned enough, he'd let a guy blow him, but that he never, to the best of his knowledge, had sex with a man. He was strictly into ladies. Any lady he chose, which was a matter of some contention between the two of them. It seems Jon was very serious last year about a particular one named Cynthia. Intended to ask her to marry him—until he found her naked in bed with Junior at one of his dinner parties, going at it with reckless abandon. He promptly dumped her and never spoke to her again."

"Must have been pissed as hell at Junior."

"You'd think so, but he insists he wasn't. Told me that it was simply a case of Junior being Junior. The man slept with anyone he wanted to, even a woman whom a good friend was serious about. Jon told me it was Cynthia he blamed, not Junior, and that the two of them remained close friends. Personally, I don't believe anyone's that big of a toady. No way he wouldn't have been furious with Junior. I would consider him a suspect. Possibly, he was with Junior when Junior stopped by the town house to pick up some of his things. Possibly, he got even by stabbing him in the eyeball with that steak knife. And, hold on, because I found out a lot more from him."

"Which is . . . ?"

"Junior shot heroin when he was in London three months ago. It seems the same social set of upper-crust Brits who get off on orgies also get off on smack."

"Do they share needles?"

"He says no. They're not dummies. But he did make a point of mentioning that Junior was the ultimate risk-taker. Did the medical examiner find any needle marks on his body?"

"He didn't. But I didn't ask him to make an extensive search for any," Golden said with a troubled look on his face. "I'll call him right now."

He got up and found the pay phone. As I finished my Scotch, a waiter went by carrying two fragrant plates of steak frites to a neighboring table. My stomach immediately started growling. I hadn't eaten since those finger sandwiches in Pippa's office.

Golden returned a few minutes later and sat back down. "Okay, he promised me he'd drop everything and search Junior's body from head to toe right away with a superpowerful lens. Told me to call him back in an hour." The lieutenant furrowed his brow. "Let's say Jon killed him . . ."

"Okay, let's."

"What were the two of them doing in the master bedroom suite together?"

"Maybe Junior went up there to wash up and Jon followed him a moment later."

"But how did he know where that box of fancy steak knives was kept?"

"Who says he did? Could be he just went rummaging around in the kitchen drawers for something sharp, and the steak knives were the first thing he found, so he grabbed a couple. Did your forensics team find any fingerprints on the kitchen drawer or the box?"

He shook his head. "It had been wiped clean. There were no prints on the handle of the steak knife either. Killer probably wore gloves." He glanced through his pocket notepad. "And they found no sign of forced entry into the house. Whoever killed him either had a set of keys or was someone like Jon—a member of Junior's inner circle."

I mulled that over before I said, "On the subject of steak knives . . ."

"What about them?"

"They serve an excellent steak frites here, and I happen to be starved. Would you be interested in eating while we continue to run this?"

"You talked me into it."

I signaled our waiter, and we ordered two steak frites, medium rare, and filet of sole for Lulu.

"And to drink?" our waiter asked.

"I'll stick with coffee," Golden said.

I ordered a Stella Artois on draft.

"Oh, hell. Make it two," Golden said as the waiter scurried off. "I still want to have a conversation with the housekeeper, Katie Healey, and her daughter, Bridget. But it's a long drive out to Rockaway Beach, so that'll have to wait until tomorrow morning."

The waiter returned with our beers, salads, and a basket filled with chunks of crusty baguette. We both dove in, munching for a moment in silence.

After I'd taken a sip of my beer, I said, "After I saw Jon, I went up to the office of SHE magazine. Pippa Longworth wants me to write a cover story on Junior, whom she considers the last of the great American gentleman adventurers. She's offering me big bucks, too."

"You going to write it?"

"Too soon to tell. I don't have a hook yet. Just for starters, I need to know who killed him, and why."

"Did you pick up anything from her?"

"That she's pissed off at Phoebe for not demanding a mammoth chunk of Junior's two hundred-million-dollar fortune in the divorce settlement."

"She got the town house, didn't she? When she sells that, she'll still end up plenty loaded. Anything else?"

"I got a not-quite-right hit off of Pippa's assistant, Tiffany Tatum. Nothing I can put my finger on. Just an instinct. She's a Yalie who's been her assistant for two years, which has to be a world record given that Pippa is a total bully. When I mentioned that to Tiffany, she just shrugged it off and said her father was a bully. She comes across very much as the SHE ideal. Smart, pretty, chic. But I kept getting the feeling that all is not what it appears to be. If I were you, I'd have someone contact the campus police chief to see if she was mixed up in anything naughty while she was there."

"Such as what?"

"Like I said, it was just an instinct."

"Lieutenant Mitry told me to pay attention to your instincts. Consider it done." He jotted it down on his notepad as our waiter arrived with our dinners. Lulu's filet of sole was placed discreetly under the table. Slurping noises ensued. Meanwhile, Golden and I began devouring our flavorful, chewy steaks and huge mounds of french fries.

"Hey, this is a good steak. I'll have to come back here sometime with Abby. Did you pick up anything else?"

"Two more solid leads from Jon. He told me that Junior has had a steady, serious thing going on for the past couple of months with Mona Dale. The Mona Dale."

"Sorry, that name means nothing to me."

"I take it you weren't a punk rocker. Four, maybe five, years ago, she was lead singer of a band called Four Hundred Blows. Had spiky pink hair, a major bod, and dressed in the slinkiest costumes you can imagine. They had one minor hit single called 'Roadkill' before they split up."

Our waiter came by, looked at our nearly empty beer glasses, and asked us if we wanted another round. I said I did. Golden said he'd better pass, then two seconds later said he did, too.

"Anyhow, I found Mona this afternoon," I said.

"No shit? How?"

"After I was done with Pippa Longworth at SHE, Lulu and I headed for that national phone book directory center on Grand Central's main concourse. I figured I'd start with the five boroughs before I tried places like L.A. and San Francisco. I got lucky. She lives on West Forty-Fifth in Hell's Kitchen."

Our waiter returned with our beers.

"So that's why you were calling me from there."

"Indeed. When I called Mona, she sounded like she was in serious mourning. I told her Junior and I were old friends, wanted her to know how sorry I was, and asked her if there was anything I could do. She told me I could pick up a cold six-pack of Pabst and come on over. As I started across the concourse toward Vanderbilt to catch a cab, I had this sudden feeling that someone was tailing me. The same kind of feeling I get late at night when I'm walking down a deserted street and am about to get mugged."

"Was someone following you?"

"Not that I could see. And Lulu, who's a world-class scent hound, didn't alert me that she'd picked up the smell of anyone with whom we'd been in recent contact. But it was a powerful feeling. When I caught a cab for Eleventh Avenue and West Forty-Fifth, I was still convinced that someone was on our tail. Not that I could spot anyone in the sea of traffic behind us. As requested, I picked up the six-pack of Pabst at the bodega on Eleventh around the corner from Mona's place. It wasn't until I walked out the door with it that Lulu suddenly came to a halt and let out a low whoop of warning. Now that we were no longer surrounded by hundreds of people in Grand Central, she'd picked up a familiar scent. And she continued to pick it up as we started toward Mona's place."

"Did you spot anyone?"

"No. Whoever it was knew how to stay out of sight. But I was definitely tailed there, and my sidekick confirmed it. Lulu's nose knows."

"Was your tail still there when you left?"

"Nope. Gone."

"Hmm . . . interesting. What's Mona's place like?"

"It's a genuine dump. Tenement basement studio with no kitchen, no shower, and plenty of mice. Furniture that she picked up on the street."

"And what about Mona?"

"Still plenty sexy, if your taste runs to sleazy and unclean, which Junior's apparently did."

"Is she on drugs? She must be."

"Actually, she can't be. Mona works behind the counter at the DMV on West Thirty-First Street, and they get drug tested."

"She works at the DMV?" he repeated in disbelief.

"That's how Junior hooked up with her. He was getting his license renewed."

"If she has a civil service job, she could afford to live in a nicer place, couldn't she?"

"That's just what I said. She said she prefers dumps because that's how she was raised. And Junior preferred to spend four or five nights a week there with her rather than in his luxury suite at the Sherry-Netherland. Jon told me that Junior liked slumming. He considered it adventuresome. And he was mad about Mona. They'd drink Pabst, eat Chinese takeout, and watch TV together. And, unlike Phoebe and Siena, she said he was a passionate lovemaker who could go all night. She also said there was another woman in his life. Someone clingy who he was trying to get rid of. She didn't know who, and swore she didn't care because he wanted to be with her, not this other woman, and that was all that mattered. Weird as it sounds, they had a deep relationship. Mona's genuinely grief-stricken. Sees no reason to stay alive now that Junior's gone."

Golden finished the last of his steak and fries, dabbed at his mouth with his napkin, and sat back in his chair. "I don't get it. You're telling me the guy's worth two hundred mil and chooses to spend his nights in a Hell's Kitchen rodent trap with an unwashed ex-punk star who works for the DMV?"

"Pay a call on her if you don't believe me. She's in the phone book."

"Did you ask her if she's HIV positive?"

"She swears not. Always insists a guy wear a condom because she picked up every sexually transmitted disease you can think of back when she was working the clubs."

"Think she has a motive for killing him?"

"I sure didn't sense one. Like I said, her grief seemed genuine. And she swore she'd never visited his town house. But she's a bundle of crazy. If your forensics team finds her prints there, then it's a whole different story."

Golden glanced at his watch. "I want to check in with the medical examiner to find out if he spotted any needle marks on Junior's body."

He got up and started back to the pay phone. I sat there with my wheels spinning, trying to get a handle on what drove Junior to behave the way he did. He was impossible to decipher. I sure couldn't imagine how I'd be able to write an in-depth profile of him. Not yet, anyhow.

Golden returned a moment later, sat back, and said, "Bingo. He found minute traces of four hypodermic marks between the big toe and second toe of Junior's right foot. Based on the healed condition of the marks, his best guess was that Junior was shooting heroin as recently as two weeks ago. If he was sharing a needle with someone, that could explain how he picked up the virus."

I ordered an espresso from our waiter.

Golden did, too, then sat there furrowing his brow thoughtfully. "If he wasn't shooting up with Mona, then we have to find out who his other lover was."

"Who says it was a lover?"

"Speak English, man."

"I told you I had two more solid leads from Jon. One was Mona. The other was that Junior had a taste for Black streetwalkers. I'm talking hot pants, fishnet hose, and go-go boots. He liked to frequent a strip of sidewalk on Broadway between West Eighty-Sixth and Eighty-Seventh. The Sloan's supermarket that's there closes at eight. Once it does, they go to work."

Golden nodded. "Sure, I know it. Strutters' Walk."

"Indeed," I said as our waiter returned with our espressos. I sipped mine. "The girls either get picked up for rides by suburbanites who've driven into town to get their rocks off or they avail themselves of the parked cars in the four-story garage around the corner on West Eighty-Seventh between Broadway and West End. There's a teeny-tiny mystery bookstore squeezed in between the garage's entrance and exit called Murder Ink. While readers are browsing for books, the hookers are getting it on upstairs in parked cars with their johns. They shmear the garage attendants by giving them freebies. Their pimps and dealers hang out nearby at Pick 'n' Pay, a twenty-four-hour bodega on the northeast corner of Broadway and West Eighty-Seventh that caters strictly to a creepy clientele. You'd swear that everyone in there has bulging purple eyeballs."

He studied me curiously. "You sound pretty familiar with the scene."

"I still have my unheated fifth-floor walk-up in a brownstone on West Ninety-Third between West End and Riverside. Not the greatest neighborhood. I spent three whole years there writing my novel, day and night, and another year rewriting it after I sold it. Ever since I moved in with Merilee, I'm hardly there anymore, except to collect my mail. But I've still got all of my books, summer clothes, and other stuff there, and the rent's only two hundred and twenty-five bucks a month, so I'm holding on to it until we buy a place together. When I was working on my book, I hardly ever went out except to stock up on provisions at Williams, the holy temple of rotisserie chickens that's across Broadway from Sloan's. And there's a liquor store next to Sloan's that has good cheap wine. After I'd stock up, I'd stroll back home. Trade jokes with the girls. The garage attendants always had the Mets or Knicks on the radio, depending on the season. I'd ask them what the score was, and we'd exult or curse. And if I was afraid I'd run out of Chesterfields in the middle of the night, I'd stop off at the Pick 'n' Pay."

"You still a smoker?"

"Nope. I quit."

"Me, too. Abby insisted on it. Hates the smell. Wasn't easy, let me tell you. I wouldn't have done it for anyone except her." Golden drained his espresso. "Did Jon know whether Junior had a favorite sidewalk strutter?"

"He didn't share that information with me, leading me to believe Junior never mentioned it. I'm planning to head up there tonight to find out."

Golden shook his head at me. "Not by yourself, you're not."

"It's still my neighborhood. I'm not worried."

"Maybe you're not, but I am. You're not going up there to buy a rotisserie chicken. You'll be asking whores, pimps, and smack dealers questions having to do with a violent homicide. If anyone so much as touches a hair on your head, my career is toast. So wherever you go, I go."

"Do you really think that's necessary?"

"I don't think it. I know it. I won't cramp your style. I worked undercover for five years. You won't even know I'm there."

"Well, okay," I said as I signaled for the check. "But I forget, which one of us is Starsky and which one is Hutch?"

"Tell you what," Golden said. "I'll leave that one up to you."

CHAPTER NINE

The girls on Strutters' Walk would have spotted Golden's cruiser right away and scattered, so he dropped Lulu and me off at West Eighty-Fifth and Amsterdam. He'd given me his copy of that morning's *Daily News*. I'd used the miniature scissors on my Swiss Army knife to cut Junior's picture out and put it in the pocket of my trench coat.

As my four-legged sidekick and I got out, Golden said, "You won't see me, but I'll be nearby. Just do me a favor and don't do anything reckless or stupid."

"I'll try my best."

I started toward Broadway on West Eighty-Sixth, inhaling the oh-so-wonderful fragrance of Williams' rotisserie chickens. They stayed open late. Sloan's didn't. The lights in the supermarket were dimmed, and the girls, eight or ten of them, were out on the sidewalk in their short fake-fur coats, hot pants, fishnet hose, and go-go boots. All of them were Black except for the two who were Latinas. A car slowed down, and the driver gestured to one of the Latinas, who sashayed over, talked to him through his open window for a second, and got in. As they drove away, I spotted Golden going into the liquor store next door, just like any anonymous-looking businessman in a rumpled overcoat buying a bottle of something. That was the last I saw of him as Lulu and I strolled our way past the perfume-soaked girls.

"I got what you be looking for, handsome!" one of them called out to me.

Another made kissy-kissy noises at me. "Love your puppy, baby. What's her name?"

"Lulu."

"She's precious."

Lulu grunted sourly. She hates to be called precious.

We continued our way along Strutters' Walk, not too fast, not too slow. Lulu started to sneeze from all of the cheap, heavy perfume in the air. She's allergic to it.

"What's a stud like you doing out all by yourself on a cold night?" one of them asked me. "Need some company?"

"I know how to make you warm all over," the girl next to her assured me.

When we'd made our way past them, I crossed West Eighty-Seventh, made a left, and started toward West End. The four-story garage was halfway down the block. Murder Ink was closed for the night, but the well-lit window displayed new mysteries by Ross Thomas and Donald Westlake. I took the driveway into the garage, where a familiar fifty-something Black attendant in overalls was listening to the Knicks game on the radio.

I grinned at him. "How are we doing?" I called out to him like always.

"Aw, down by six in the third quarter to the fucking Bucks," he answered disgustedly. "How's it going, my man? Ain't seen you lately."

"Moved in with a girl who lives in the Village. Her place has heat."

"Hell, I'd marry her if I was you. This must be her pup." He bent down and patted Lulu affectionately. "You didn't used to have one, did you?"

"Nope, just roaches."

He let out a cackle, becoming aware now that I was lingering. "Help you out with something?"

"Maybe. Buddy of mine bailed on his wife. Hasn't come home since last week. She's getting worried. He used to be a regular here," I said, raising my eyes upward to where the cars were parked. I pulled Junior's photo from the pocket of my trench coat along with a ten-dollar bill, which disappeared instantly.

"Sure, I recognize him. Likes him one particular girl named Chantelle."

"Has he been around this week?"

He frowned. "Naw, not for a couple of weeks. Maybe more. Neither has Chantelle. Dunno why."

I glanced in the direction of the Pick 'n' Pay. "Who would know why?"

"Breeze is who you want. Big, heavy guy. Wears a blue down jacket."

I slipped him another ten. "Thanks."

"No big. That is one fine puppy. What's her name?"

"Lulu."

"Like Ed Norton's dog from *The Honeymooners*?"

"You're a fan?"

"Hell yeah. Who ain't?"

We walked back toward Broadway and crossed the street to the Pick 'n' Pay corner, where a half-dozen Black guys were leaning against two parked cars, smoking cigarettes, and pretending they weren't doing business. I felt an uptick in my pulse, well aware that most, if not all, of them were armed.

"Breeze?" I called out to the big, heavy one in the blue down jacket. Big and heavy didn't begin to describe him. Huge was more like it. He had to be six feet four and 275 pounds easily.

"And what can I do for you, my man?" he responded, giving me the impression he was jolly, which I felt quite certain he was not.

"Get me out of trouble."

"Sorry, that ain't what I do. But if you want to get into trouble, I'm your man," he said with a laugh. Two of the guys standing next to him laughed and slapped meat with him.

The twenty I offered him disappeared into his hand. "Last week, a buddy of mine bailed on his wife."

"Uh-huh. And I'm supposed to give a shit because . . . ?"

As I was about to answer, I noticed a middle-aged businessman in a rumpled topcoat go inside the Pick 'n' Pay to buy a Baby Ruth. Lieutenant Golden was taking no chances.

"He once told me he had a thing for one of your girls, Chantelle." I showed Breeze Junior's *Daily News* photo.

He squinted at it in the light from the bodega's window. "Yeah, I seen him. So?"

"I was wondering if Chantelle might have seen him lately. Would you mind pointing her out to me? I'd like to ask her."

He handed the photo back to me. "Can't help you. Chantelle ain't been around for two, three weeks. She's got the flu. Nasty cough, looks like shit. Ain't no guy wants to get with a girl when she's that sick. I sent her home. She been crashing with her moms at the Lincoln Projects."

"What's Chantelle's last name?"

He stuck his chin out at me, which officially ended the jolly act. "You a cop?"

"Do I look like a cop?"

"You don't, but your dog does." He and his pals had another good laugh before he said, "Williams. Chantelle Williams."

"Thanks. Appreciate it."

"No big."

I started to walk away, then stopped. "Being honest, my buddy has himself a problem."

He narrowed his gaze at me. "What kind of problem we talking about?"

"He likes to shoot smack. Do he and Chantelle shoot up together?"

"What if they do?" a different voice answered. A low, hostile voice that belonged to a Black guy leaning against the other of the two cars. Unlike Breeze, he looked lean and mean. Wore a black leather jacket and had a knife-scarred face.

"My buddy's HIV positive," I said. "He has the AIDS virus. If he and Chantelle shared a needle, then she has it, too."

"Move on out of here, man." He pulled a switch-blade out of his jacket pocket and flicked it open with lightning quickness. "And I mean now."

Breeze patted me on the shoulder. "Do what Ray-Ray says. And don't stress. Your buddy will get better."

"You don't get better from AIDS. You die."

Ray-Ray sidled over toward me and held the point of the knife to my throat. Lulu immediately let out a growl of warning.

He glanced down at her. "Ferocious, huh?"

"Just protective," I said in as calm a voice as I could muster.

"I told you to move on. Move on."

"I'll be doing that. Thank you both for your time."

I heard low, angry murmuring behind me as Lulu and I started walking away. When we went around the corner of the building, I realized that Golden had been standing less than ten feet away with his jacket unbuttoned and his .357 Magnum unholstered.

"Enjoy your Baby Ruth?" I asked him as we headed back toward his cruiser on Amsterdam.

"Immensely. You seem to be in one piece. He didn't nick you, did he?"

"Nope. He was just trying to scare me."

"Did he succeed?"

"Yeah, he did a pretty fair job."

He unlocked his cruiser, and we got in. Lulu yawned and stretched out between us with her head in my lap. She was still a puppy, and it had been a long day for her. Not a single decent nap.

Golden sat there staring out the windshield at the street. "I only caught bits and pieces of what you guys were saying. Want to run what you know for me?"

"What I don't know is whether Junior was an insane risk-taker or simply had a death wish, but he used to shoot heroin in a parked car in that garage with a strutter named Chantelle Williams, who's been out sick for at least two weeks with the flu, according to her pimp, Breeze. As you may have noticed, Chantelle's dealer, the very pleasant knife-wielding Ray-Ray, didn't wish to pursue the conversation any further. Chantelle is staying in the Lincoln Projects with her mom. If Junior and Chantelle shared needles, which I surmise that they did, then he got the AIDS virus from her and then passed it on to Siena."

"Did you just say surmise?"

"I did. Why?"

"Don't hear that word very often."

"Then you need to work with a higher class of people. Which you will once you crack this case."

Lulu began to snore.

He gazed down at her fondly. "I guess it's time to take you two home."

"I guess it is."

He started the engine but didn't go anywhere. Just sat there, idling. "I still want to talk to Phoebe's maid, Katie Healey, and her daughter, Bridget. They may know something. I'll hit Rockaway Beach in the morning."

"Makes sense," I said, stifling a yawn of my own. It had been an exhausting day, and I was feeling the aftereffects of my close encounter with Ray-Ray and his switchblade. "As for right now, let's roll."

"Let's roll?"

"I've always wanted to say that."

He complied by putting his Crown Vic in gear and speeding his way down Broadway, glancing at me with concern. "You had yourself a bit of a scare back there. Are you okay?"

"Fine and dandy. In fact, meeting Ray-Ray was the high point of my day. No, I take that back. But it ranks as a close second."

"To what?"

"Seeing Mona Dale's hairy armpits. That qualified as a once-in-a-lifetime experience."

CHAPTER TEN

It was nearly eleven by the time Golden pulled up in front of the Charlton house and idled there. Mercifully, the tabloid media had called it a night. All was quiet. "So what's up with you tomorrow?" he wanted to know.

"An early start, for one thing. My physical therapy appointment on my trapezius is at eight A.M. Lasts forty-five minutes."

"I've been meaning to ask you—exactly what happened to you?"

"That's something I'd prefer not to talk about. If you really want to know, Lieutenant Mitry will fill you in, although something tells me he'd prefer not to talk about it, either."

He looked at me curiously. "Okay . . ."

"After my PT, I'm hoping to arrange an interview with Dr. Jill Perlo for the SHE article on Junior, the last of America's gentleman adventurers, which I may or may not write."

"Jill Perlo . . ." Golden furrowed his brow. "Isn't she that nutjob scientist who keeps telling everyone that the planet is getting so hot that it will no longer be able to sustain human life?"

"She's the top climatologist in America, and she knows what she's talking about. People think she's a nutjob because they don't want to hear what she has to say. She and Junior got into a nasty tiff at the Lunch Club last week, and she stormed out. I'd like to find out what they were arguing about."

"She a looker?"

"Most definitely. A lean, fit blonde in her early thirties. Also an expert rock climber."

"Think they were romantically involved?"

"Wouldn't surprise me."

"I wonder if she's somebody who I should be looking at, steak-knife-in-the-eyeball-wise."

"I'll be sure to let you know after I touch base with her."

"Know how to reach her?"

"Not yet, as a matter of fact."

"She might have an unlisted number. I'll track it down for you and call you in the morning."

"I'd appreciate that. Thanks." I roused Lulu and started to get out of the car.

"Not so fast. I'll want a favor in return."

"What is it?"

"Take that ride out to Rockaway Beach with me to talk to Katie Healey and her daughter, Bridget."

"Any particular reason why?"

"You might get a read on them that I don't. You have keen insights, or so I've surmised. Deal?"

"Deal."

"Great. Until tomorrow. Good night, Lulu," he said as she got out of the cruiser with me. Then he sped off into the night.

I took her for a brief bedtime walk before we went inside. The kitchen and stairway lights were on, and the living room was dark. There was a dim light under the master bedroom door, and the guest bedroom at the top of the stairs was dark. I turned off the kitchen light and started up the stairs with Lulu, who was getting better at climbing but was so tuckered out I picked her up, carried her to our bedroom, and quietly opened the door. Merilee's nightstand lamp was on, and she was dozing with a film script on the chest of her red flannel nightshirt. The embers from the fireplace still warmed the room. I stood there smiling. It was a welcome sight to come home to.

I put Lulu down on the bed. She licked Merilee's face and wriggled around, happy to see her.

Merilee stirred, stroking her. "It's my sweetness," she said sleepily. "Did you happen to bring a tall guy home with you? Oh, there he is. You look exhausted, darling."

"Only because I am."

"And I would swear you smell of cheap perfume."

"Only because I do. I'll bundle up this suit and send it off to the cleaners. Right now, I desperately need to take a hot shower."

"Wait, I want to hear about your day."

"Just give me two minutes first. How's Phoebe?"

"The good news is that the results of her HIV blood test were negative. She's fine."

"That is good news. She must be relieved. What's the bad news?"

"She was asked to pay a call at Brearley after our pair of sturdy patrolmen helped her clear her things out of Meredith's apartment. Meredith informed her that the head of school wished to see her."

"That doesn't sound good."

"It most definitely was not. She was told that it would be best for her, and for Brearley, for her to 'put her affairs in order.' Which is to say they can't maintain their high-class reputation if they're associated with anything scandalous."

"Did they ask her to take a leave of absence?"

"They did. In fact, Phoebe thinks that when the dust settles, she'll be asked to look for a new job. She's hanging on by her fingernails, poor thing. It did not help that Pippa phoned her three times tonight demanding she move in with her."

"Yeah, that would be just the calming influence Phoebe needs. How about Barry the Eye Doctor? Did he invite her to move in with him, too?"

"Hardly. He went Claude Rains on her. She had to call him. He said he was with a patient and would call her right back—which he did two hours later. He confessed he's afraid that if she moves in with him that he'll get drawn into all of the tabloid attention that Junior's murder is getting. His patients wouldn't like that. They expect total confidentiality. So, under the circumstances, he didn't think it would be advisable."

"What a dick. I hope she dumped him."

"She did, as a matter of fact. Told him if he genuinely cared about her that none of that would matter, and that she never wanted to hear from him again."

"Good for Phoebe."

"So, starting first thing tomorrow morning, all she needs is a new job, a new apartment, a new chamber music group, and a new boyfriend."

"She's better off without him. He's a two-timing putz. He's lucky she didn't take a cab up to his apartment and punch him in the face. Although that's not her style, I suppose."

"I never suppose anything with Phoebe. We've been like sisters our whole lives, but she keeps her feelings to herself."

"I find her hard to read, too. The only thing I know for sure about her is that she has lousy taste in men."

"I'm afraid so. Go take your shower so you can tell me where you've been. But please hurry. I need for you to hold me."

I stripped off my suit, opened the bedroom door, and threw it down the stairs along with my shirt. My shoes went in the closet, my Sex Pistols T-shirt, boxers, and socks in the laundry hamper. I took a steaming shower and shampooed my hair twice. After I dried off, I got into bed naked with the love of my life, who'd turned off her nightstand lamp and taken off her red flannel nightshirt. I never stopped marveling over how smooth her skin was. Buried my nose in her neck and inhaled the scent of her as Lulu snored softly at the foot of the bed.

"Hold me, darling. Don't let go."

"No chance of that, Blond Person."

She let out a sigh that was almost but not quite a purr. "Okay, tell me what's happened."

"Siena Bing, Realtor to the rich, tested HIV positive two weeks ago. It seems she had an unprotected quickie with Junior when he stopped by the house to pick up some of his things. She was plenty willing. He was great-looking and famous, although a five-minute man in the sack. Lousy kisser, too."

"Lousy as in . . . ?"

"Too much tongue."

"Yech."

"It seems the only person with whom he had great sex was Mona Dale. She told me they'd go at it all night."

"Mona Dale, as in Four Hundred Blows Mona Dale?"

"The same. And she's still plenty sexy, provided you aren't put off by smelly feet."

"How on earth did Junior meet her?"

"In line at the DMV on Eleventh Avenue. She works there now."

"You're kidding."

"Am not. Junior's friend Jon tipped me off about her. She lives in a dive basement studio apartment in Hell's Kitchen. For the past two months, she and Junior have been having passionate sex there four or five nights a week. Couldn't get enough of each other."

"Did they shoot heroin together?"

"She swears no. The DMV drug tests her. But Golden double-checked with the medical examiner, and Junior had indeed been shooting heroin. He found minute traces of hypodermic marks."

"Was it Mona who reeked of that cheap perfume?"

"No, the source of that was significantly lower on the food chain. I also found out from Jon that Junior liked to go slumming on Strutters' Walk, which is what they call the stretch of sidewalk where the hookers in hot pants and go-go boots shake their booties after nine o'clock in front of the Sloan's market in my old neighborhood. I used to see them there all of the time. They turned tricks in the parked cars in the garage around the corner on West Eighty-Seventh. One of the attendants there remembered me. He always had a ball game blaring on the radio when I walked by, and we'd talk sports. I showed him a photo of Junior that I'd cut out of the newspaper and asked him if he recognized him. He said he hadn't seen him for a while but that he liked to share a back seat with Chantelle pretty regularly. When I asked him if Chantelle was around, he said he hadn't seen her for a while, either. Directed me to Breeze, her pimp, who hangs out with the other pimps and drug dealers outside of the Pick 'n' Pay twenty-four-hour bodega on Broadway and Eighty-Seventh. A truly classy place. You'd love it."

"Excuse me, darling, but was Lieutenant Golden with you, or were you by yourself? Because you're starting to scare me."

"Not to worry. He hovered nearby. Besides, I had my protector." Lulu was so fast asleep that her tail didn't thump. "When I asked Breeze if Chantelle was around, he said she was home sick with her mom in the Lincoln Projects. He wanted to know why I was asking. I told him my wife's cousin is married to a dirtbag who's disappeared on her. Showed him Junior's picture. He said he'd seen him around. I said he had a taste for smack and wondered if he and Chantelle shot up together. Right away, the drug dealer standing next to him suggested I move on. So Lulu and I moved on, mission accomplished."

"Meaning Junior picked up the AIDS virus from Chantelle?"

"Sure appears that way." I chose to omit the part about Ray-Ray pulling his switchblade knife on me. There was no sense in freaking Merilee out. "Then Lieutenant Golden drove us home, and now there is absolutely no need for me to leave this bed."

"Good." Merilee rolled over on top of me and hugged me tightly. "Would you like to know what I love best about you, mister?"

"Do tell."

"That you're not a five-minute man."

CHAPTER ELEVEN

It was Merilee who took Lulu for her predawn walk in the morning because she and Phoebe intended to take a 7:00 A.M. yoga class before the media horde descended on the Charlton house. I was still fast asleep when Merilee awakened me with a steaming-hot double espresso and Lulu climbed back onto the bed to join me, her breath redolent of 9Lives mackerel. Yawning, I propped up my pillows, sat up, and took a grateful gulp while Lulu rolled around on her back, waiting for me to give her a belly rub.

"Good morning," Phoebe said to me with surprisingly good cheer through the open doorway. She even teased me a bit about my bare chest. "Nice pecs. I thought writers were supposed to have sunken chests and no muscle tone at all."

I covered myself with the blanket and said, "You forget I was an intercollegiate track star."

She looked at Merilee blankly. "He was?"

"He most certainly was. He was the third best javelin hurler in the entire Ivy League."

"Not to mention first alternate on our mile relay team," I added.

"I had no idea," she confessed.

"That's because I don't like to brag."

Merilee said, "We're out of here, darling. And we're planning to stop for breakfast after class to draw up our to-do list. If you have your eight o'clock PT at Lenox Hill today, you'd better not lollygag. See you later?"

"If I'm not here when you get back, I'll call when I can. How is it out?"

"Drizzly." She kissed me, Phoebe waved goodbye, and they headed downstairs.

I did lollygag for a minute or two, finishing my coffee before I got up, brushed my teeth, stropped Grandfather's razor, lathered up, and shaved. I stowed my sweatshirt, sweatpants, and ancient black high-top Chuck Taylor All Stars in my gym bag and dressed in my Buster Poindexter T-shirt, navy blue cashmere turtleneck sweater, gray herringbone tweed jacket, charcoal flannel slacks, and Gore-Tex street walkers. When I went downstairs, Lulu plop-plopping close behind me, I discovered that Lieutenant Golden had left me a phone message while I was shaving. It was Jill Perlo's phone number and address on Christopher Street in the West Village. When the man said he'd take care of something for me, he took care of it. It was only 7:30, as in too early for me to call her. Besides, I needed to scoot if I was going to make it up to Lenox Hill Hospital for my PT by 8:00. I put on my trench coat and fedora, hooked Lulu to her leash, and out the door we went. Only a few half-awake reporters, photographers, and local TV news cameras had arrived, and they showed little interest in me. The blondes. They wanted the blondes.

I hailed a cab and off we went.

◆

"You're killing it, Hoagy!" Angela, my gung ho, frizzy-haired physical therapist, exulted at the top of her lungs as I worked the shoulder rotation machine, which she'd adjusted for an incredible amount of resistance. Sweat was pouring off me after five minutes, and I still had fifteen minutes to go. Lulu was having a much easier time of it jogging on the treadmill. "You're the man!"

When the timer mercifully buzzed, I eased to a halt, gasping, and climbed off.

She toweled my left shoulder and trapezius muscles dry and wrapped the entire area in a huge ice pack. "I swear, you are almost completely there in the strength department. Do you feel any difference between the two shoulders?"

"It's . . . very slight," I responded, catching my breath.

"What about pain?"

"It's not bad at all. I'm not even taking Tylenol anymore."

"You are killing it!"

"Would you mind using a different choice of words?"

"I'd say two more sessions and we're done, though I want you to keep swimming three times a week."

"I can do that."

"Give me a high five!"

I gave her a high five, then watched her slow down Lulu's treadmill so that Lulu could step off, panting a bit.

"This'll do her a world of good with those short legs of hers," Angela explained as she put down a dish of water. Lulu lapped it up thirstily. "One thing you never, ever want is a fat basset hound. Her tummy will scrape against the ground. It's not a good look, believe me."

"Angela, I've never doubted you for a minute."

◆

Merilee and Phoebe were still out when I got home. I called the number Golden had given me for Dr. Jill Perlo. It went to her answering machine. I left her a message with my name and number, said that it concerned Junior Singleton, and asked her to please call me back. She did, within thirty seconds. Clearly, she monitored her calls.

"This is Jill Perlo, Mr. Hoag."

"It's Hoagy."

"We've met at the Lunch Club, haven't we? You're the one who's the first major new literary voice of the nineteen eighties."

"Or words to that effect. Yes. That is to say, I'm a member of the Lunch Club and we have spoken briefly."

"Were you and Junior friends?"

"College classmates. And his ex-wife, Phoebe, is my wife's cousin." I was still getting used to hearing the words 'my wife' come out of my own mouth.

"Junior told me that Phoebe's cousin is Merilee Nash. You're married to her?"

"Yes. We got married the same morning that we found Junior's body in the dressing room of the town house. Phoebe has put the place on the market and was hoping we'd buy it, which, believe me, will never happen now. I still can't shake the image of that steak knife in his eyeball."

"You will. Your survival instinct will kick in very soon. Now that we've got all of that cleared up, exactly what is it you want?"

"I was wondering if we could have a talk about Junior."

"Whatever for?" she asked with a testy edge in her voice.

"The editor of SHE magazine, who happens to be Phoebe's mother, wants me to write a cover story on him. She considers him the last of the great American gentleman adventurers. Could we get a cup of coffee or take a walk?"

"When?"

"Whenever is convenient."

"Now is convenient. Where are you, Hoagy?"

"Charlton Street."

"I can meet you under the arch in Washington Square Park in, say, twenty minutes. Would that work?"

"Perfectly. See you then." After I hung up, I called Lieutenant Golden and told him if he still wanted me to head out to Rockaway Beach with him that he should park outside of the One Fifth Avenue building in one hour or thereabouts, and I'd meet him there.

He was cool with that.

◆

It doesn't matter whether it's winter, spring, summer, or fall, Washington Square always bustles with people—students going to and from classes at NYU, out-of-work musicians strumming on guitars, aspiring authors poring over well-thumbed paperback novels, apartment hunters searching the classifieds in the *Voice,* loiterers loitering, chatterers chattering. It's the heart of Greenwich Village.

On this drizzly January morning, I found Dr. Jill Perlo pacing impatiently under the landmark arch even though Lulu and I were right on time. Her hands were stuffed in the pockets of a mountaineering parka that was so well worn it was patched with silver duct tape. She wore a wool stocking cap over her chin-length blond hair, jeans, and hiking boots.

She nodded with recognition when she saw me and stuck out her hand. Men are taught to shake a woman's hand gently if she offers it. Her grip was so strong she nearly made me wince. Her pale blue eyes were piercing. Her squarish jaw was stuck out challengingly. The brilliant climate scientist bristled with intensity. She glanced down at my short-legged partner but didn't pet her or offer a comment. Didn't believe in wasting time.

As we began to walk briskly around the circular fountain that anchored Washington Square, she said, "You mentioned on the phone that SHE magazine considers Junior the last of America's gentleman adventurers. He was an adventurer all right. When we went rock climbing together in Bryce Canyon National Park, he was confident and fearless. But he was no gentleman. He was a spoiled rich kid who acted like a big baby if he didn't get his way."

"My personal feeling is that he was restless and unsettled because he had no genuine sense of purpose in life. So he climbed mountains, raced cars, flew hang gliders. He even shot heroin."

She looked at me in surprise. "He did? I had no idea."

"He shot up with a street hooker. They'd share a needle. When the medical examiner performed his autopsy, he discovered that Junior was HIV positive."

Jill shook her head in disgust. "There's a world of difference between being an adventurer and a self-destructive idiot. He was also a total bastard. When I wouldn't share my sleeping bag with him on our Bryce Canyon trip, he cut off my research funding. He'd been providing most of my financial backing for the past year. Built a state-of-the-art computer lab for me up at Canterbury College because he was interested in my climate research." Canterbury was a small, distinguished college located in the Inwood section of upper Manhattan. "It turned out that what he was really interested in was getting into my pants."

"I take it he didn't," I said as we continued to stroll around the fountain.

"I'm gay, Hoagy. I live with a woman who's a biologist at NYU. But Junior was one of those men who believe a gay woman would make an exception in his case because he's so irresistible. When he finally got it into his skull that sex was off the table, he not only cut off my funding but had a computer wiz change all of my codes and lock me out of my own research findings. I had to hire a wiz of my own to recover it before he dismantled the entire system."

"Is that what you two were arguing about at the Lunch Club?"

She frowned. "Why are you asking me about that?"

"Well, he's dead. Someone killed him."

"You don't actually think I'm that someone, do you?"

"No, but you were seen arguing with him heatedly at the Lunch Club by me and no doubt several other members. And based on what you've told me he did to your computer codes, you had every reason in the world to be furious with him. When the homicide lieutenant who's handling the case, Meyer Golden, starts asking questions at the Lunch Club, your name is going to come up and you'll immediately qualify as a person of interest."

"I did not stick a steak knife in Junior's eyeball," she said angrily. "I'm not a murderer. Besides, if I'd actually wanted to kill him, which I didn't, I'd have gone climbing with him and shoved him off a cliff. Do you climb?"

"A bit, but I suffered a serious trapezius injury in October and am still in rehab, so if you're planning to bump me off, you'll have to come up with a different strategy."

She peered at me. "You have a rather strange way of kidding."

"I'm a writer, remember? I'm pretty much all-around strange."

"Junior and I had a dispute, okay? I was very upset that he had so little respect for my sexual identity that he cut off my funding. This is important work I'm doing. He behaved like a total asshole, and I told him so." She broke off, breathing in and out angrily. "Beyond that, my opinion of him is similar to yours. He was an international daredevil because he had no real purpose in life. Nothing that he believed in. I thought he believed in my cause, and I welcomed his financial support. The traditional academic community, which is comprised mostly of gray-haired men, dismisses me because I'm a lesbian who dares to say things they don't want to hear. They consider me an alarmist kook. Trust me when I tell you I'm not. We're overdeveloping the American Southwest like mad with no long-range plan for where the water's going to come from. Americans are very stupid that way. We don't look ahead. We just assume everything will turn out all right because God loves us." She slowed to a halt, bent down, and gave Lulu some attention with an affectionate pat. "It's also impossible for the old farts to admit to themselves that I might be smarter than they are. Junior understood that. It's why he gave me the money to continue my research, no strings attached. Or so he led me to believe."

"Did he ever talk much about Phoebe?"

"He said she was beautiful, well-bred, and a total bore."

"I keep wondering why he married her. They weren't at all alike."

Jill shrugged. "Sometimes opposites fascinate each other, at least for a while. And it's obvious there were two hundred million reasons that fascinated her."

"She didn't hold out for a fraction of what she could have when she divorced him. His fortune doesn't seem to matter to her, although it mattered to that mother of hers. Pippa's still upset that Phoebe didn't hire a pit bull lawyer who would have fought tooth and nail for every million she was entitled to. Were you ever at their town house?"

"No, never." She looked at me curiously. "Why?"

"Because the forensics squad is still combing the house for fingerprints. You're sure you were never there?"

"I was never there," she said, biting off the words. "And I don't lie."

"What will you do for financial backing now?"

"Apply for grants. A friend of mine who's a molecular biologist just got excellent backing from the University of Colorado. They weren't bothered by the fact that she's a lesbian." Jill fell silent for a moment, shaking her head. "Even though Junior treated me like shit, I'm genuinely sorry about what happened to him. He was an intriguing person who thought nothing could ever possibly hurt him. Just plunged right in with a complete absence of fear. You don't make it to the top of Everest twice if you have any fear." She glanced at me curiously. "He really shot heroin with a street hooker?"

"He really did. Numerous times."

"It makes no sense. None at all."

"I agree. Not unless, deep down inside, he had a death wish."

Dr. Jill Perlo let that sink in for a moment. "A death wish," she said, nodding her head before she strode off without saying goodbye.

◆

Lieutenant Golden hadn't arrived yet at One Fifth Avenue, so I phoned home from a pay phone.

"I'm glad you caught me, darling." Merilee sounded a bit out of breath. "My day has taken an unexpected turn. Robert Altman's assistant just phoned. He's in town and wants to meet with me at his agency to see how we get along, which is very important to him. Elliott Gould will be joining us. He's an Altman favorite. I've always wanted to work with him, and Altman has an idea he thinks will be perfect for the two of us."

"This sounds very exciting, Merilee."

"Doesn't it? His assistant warned me that we'll probably keep talking right on through dinner at Elaine's. I'm afraid that means Phoebe's going to be all alone here until you get back. Any idea when that will be?"

"Not really, but I'll try to get back so she isn't alone this evening. I'll take her out to dinner. Will she be okay all day by herself?"

"She insists that she will be. She wants to go up to Brearley, clear out her stuff, and say goodbye to her friends there. Then she intends to clean our house from top to bottom to pay for her keep, as she put it.

And she's been neglecting her violin and wants to practice for at least two hours."

"I hope you have fun with Altman."

"My understanding is no one actually has fun with Altman but that it's always an interesting experience. We shall see."

Golden's beat-up cruiser pulled up across the street, then in front of One Fifth Avenue.

"Ah, here's the lieutenant. Gotta run. I love you, Blondie."

"Ditto, Tall Guy. Scrunch Lulu's ears for me, will you?"

I promised I would and jaywalked across Fifth Avenue so Lulu and I could hop into Lieutenant Golden's cruiser, where he sat waiting with his engine idling. Lulu took her spot between us, her tail thumping happily.

Golden floored it from Fifth Avenue over to Third, then made a left and sped uptown. "So what did you pick up from our climate scientist?"

"Junior became so fascinated by her controversial theories after talking to her at the Lunch Club that he endowed a major computer lab for her up at Canterbury College. And when he found out she was an avid rock climber, they went climbing together in Bryce

Canyon out in Utah. He was an excellent climber, she said. Utterly fearless. The man did climb to the top of Everest twice, let us not forget. But, Junior being Junior, it turned out that what he was really most interested in was sharing her sleeping bag. She explained to him that she's gay and said no. Junior resented her rejection so deeply that he not only pulled her funding but also locked her out of her computer system."

"Sounds like a damned good reason for her to stick a knife in his eye."

"Indeed, although she swore to me she would never have done anything like that."

"What would she . . . ?"

"Invite him to go rock climbing again and shove him off a cliff."

He thumbed his jaw in silence for a moment. "Think she's in play?"

"Oh, most definitely."

Golden sped past Gramercy Park and across East Twenty-Third Street toward Kips Bay, where he made a right onto First Avenue en route to East Thirty-Sixth Street and our descent into the dimly lit hellmouth known as the Queens-Midtown Tunnel, which goes underneath the East River. Believe me, it's best not to think about it when you're experiencing it.

"I have someone else for us who might be in play," he informed me, keeping his eyes straight ahead while we were in the tunnel.

"Does that mean there's an 'us'?"

"Figure of speech," he grumbled.

"Are you going to tell me who it is or leave me in subterranean suspense?"

"We picked up some interesting info on Tiffany Tatum, Pippa Longworth's assistant at SHE. How did you know that she's a wrongo?"

"Just a hunch."

"Well, it was spot on. One of my men had a phone conversation with Yale's campus police chief. He remembers Tiffany quite well. During her junior year, she was accused of stealing the rough draft of a classmate's English Literature term paper from out of her dorm room. The classmate's basis for the accusation was that the term paper Tiffany turned in was virtually identical to her own. Their professor spoke to them privately in his office and demanded an explanation. Tiffany denied doing any such thing and said, in fact, the shoe was on the other foot. Since there was no way of knowing the truth, the professor asked them to submit new term papers on an entirely different subject. He gave Tiffany's classmate an A on hers. She's now in her third year at Yale's law school, by the way. He gave Tiffany a failing grade on hers. He felt certain it was she who stole her classmate's term paper draft and went so far as to discuss the matter with the police chief. But there wasn't enough proof to pursue the matter criminally, which is to say no classmates came forward and said they actually saw Tiffany enter the dorm room and make off with the draft. Tiffany was given a choice of flunking the class or quietly leaving school, which is what she did in the middle of her junior year."

"So she attended Yale but is not a Yale graduate."

"Correct. Her mother, who's a socialite friend of Pippa Longworth's, arranged a summer internship for her at SHE, which led to a full-time job as Pippa's personal assistant. I can't see how she factors into our investigation yet, but Lieutenant Mitry sure was right. I wish more of my detectives got hunches the way you do. What's your secret?"

"I just have a very sick mind," I said, gazing out the window with relief as we emerged from the tunnel back into drizzly daylight in Queens, where Golden got onto the Long Island Expressway, commonly known as the LIE. Once you're in Queens, you're no longer in what most of America thinks of as New

York City, or "The City" as outer borough residents call it. You're in a sprawling world of factories and working-class residential enclaves, no different from the blue-collar belt of any other grimy, aging Northeastern city. "Did you call Katie Healey to tell her we're coming?"

"No, it's best if you make a cold call on people so you catch them unprepared."

"What if she's not home?"

"I guarantee you she'll be home, parked in front of the TV watching either a soap opera or a Bette Davis movie," Golden said with total certainty. "If by some slim chance she's not, it just means she had to go to the store to buy beer and will be back in five minutes."

"You sound awfully sure about it."

"I've been doing this for a while."

"What are you hoping to find out from her?"

"Not only her but her daughter Bridget. They have a set of keys to the town house. Come and go three days a week. In my experience, they'll know plenty about what's been going on around there."

He got off the LIE and onto the Van Wyck and took that to the Cross Bay Boulevard South exit, which led us to the Cross Bay Bridge to Rockaway, the narrow beach community that had been a stronghold of Irish Americans for over a hundred years and was home to more cops and firemen per square mile than anywhere else in the five boroughs. It was commonly known as Rockaway Beach, or if you were a Ramones fan, as Rock-Rock-Rockaway Beach.

I'd been out here once before on my Norton Commando on a blazing hot summer day back when I was still with Reggie. We'd jumped into the Atlantic and swam, drank beer on the boardwalk, and people watched the crowds of muscle-bound, crew cut young firemen and their chubby-thighed, big-boobed, bikini-clad girlfriends. There were plenty of bars, delis, and small markets to be found in the commercial district. The residential district seemed to consist mostly of small, wood-framed apartment houses, four units to a building. There were narrow aprons of driveway between the apartment houses, where the older ladies who had no desire to show off their flabby selves in bathing suits sat on plastic lawn chairs in shorts and T-shirts, smoking cigarettes, drinking beer, and trading gossip. It all had a time warp feel to it, as if we'd gone back to the 1950s.

That had been a hot summer day. This was a chilly January one. The commercial district seemed deserted, and no one was sitting on lawn chairs in the driveways between those wood-framed apartment houses. The Atlantic was roiling, and what had been a drizzle when I was strolling around Washington Square Park with Dr. Jill Perlo was now a windblown rain.

"We're looking for Rockaway Park, Beach Ninety-Fifth Street," Golden said as he eased his way slowly along. When he found their address, he parked and shut off his engine. "Oh, hey, I have another piece of news for you. One of my sergeants tracked down Chantelle Williams at her mom's place. She's a full-fledged heroin addict. Has track marks up and down her arms. She hooks to pay for her habit."

"Did he get her HIV tested?"

"Sure did, and she came up positive. The odds are overwhelming that she gave Junior the virus when they shot up together."

"Does that lead you anywhere in regard to the steak knife in his eyeball?"

"I can't think of a motive for why she'd have killed him. And if those Pick 'n' Pay charmers Breeze and Ray-Ray were involved, they would have stolen everything in the house that wasn't nailed down. Nope, it's just another piece of the puzzle."

"There are getting to be an awful lot of pieces to this puzzle, Lieutenant."

"Yeah, I noticed that, too."

The wood-framed apartment house that Katie and Bridget Healey lived in was painted dark green. The building wasn't locked, so we just strolled in. Their apartment was on the second floor. As we approached the door, I heard the TV blaring. There was no mistaking the voice of the actress who was speaking. It was Bette Davis.

"Damn, you're good," I said.

"I have my moments," Golden acknowledged as he knocked on the door.

"Come on in," a woman hollered to us. She didn't bother to ask who we were. It was a neighborhood where everybody knew everybody.

We went on in. The living room was small, low ceilinged, and furnished for summer, not winter. Cotton rugs and curtains. Canvas upholstery. It wasn't overly warm in there. There wasn't much in the way of insulation. But it had a nice picture window view of the boardwalk and the ocean beyond it. There was an eat-in kitchen and a doorway that led to the bedrooms and bath. Lulu made a quick lap around the living room and kitchen before she stretched out on the cotton rug that was set before the sofa in front of the picture window.

Katie, who sat in a well-worn recliner engrossed in her Bette Davis movie—it was *The Letter* in case you're wondering—paid no attention to Lulu at all. And barely any attention to Golden and me. Her eyes didn't leave the TV screen. She was a chunky woman with frizzy white hair and a nose that was starting to turn purple, possibly because she was drinking a can of Ballantine Ale and it wasn't lunchtime yet. I've never understood how anyone can drink Ballantine. It tastes remarkably like sudsy dishwater. She was wearing a heavy cardigan sweater, wool slacks, and carpet slippers. After a moment, a long moment, a high-decibel commercial for Crazy Eddie, the discount electronics chain, came on.

She muted the sound with her remote control and looked up at us standing there. "You fellas selling something? Because whatever it is, I'm not buying it."

"Actually, I'm Detective Lieutenant Meyer Golden of the NYPD. I'm investigating Junior Singleton's murder. Would you mind turning off the TV?"

She complied, her mouth tightening. "I figured you'd want to talk to me. Awful business. Just awful. I sharpened those steak knives every two weeks. Such a beautiful set of knives. I still can't believe one of them was used on Junior." She glanced at me. "You his sergeant?"

"No, I'm Stewart Hoag. I found Junior's body. I was looking at the house with my wife, who's Phoebe's cousin. Phoebe was eager for us to buy it, although not anymore."

Katie nodded her frizzy white head. "Of course not. After what you saw, you could never live there." She wagged a short, chubby finger at me. "Phoebe's cousin is Merilee Nash, the movie star."

Lulu let out a little whimper at the mention of her mommy's name.

Katie whirled and peered at her in surprise. "Where'd that puppy come from?"

"She belongs to Merilee and me."

"So you're really married to her?"

"I really am. Have been since Tuesday morning, although things haven't exactly gone the way we planned. We've had to delay our honeymoon, and Phoebe is living with us for now."

"I hope you're not about to say a word against Phoebe in front of me," Katie said.

"Wouldn't occur to me to. I like Phoebe a lot."

"I'm glad to hear you say that, because she's cream and sugar as far as I'm concerned. A real lady. Gracious, polite, puts on no airs. And, let me tell you, when my hip started bothering me a few months back, she made an appointment for me with her doctor. He gave me a cortisone shot and told me to rest a bit more, so my daughter, Bridget, started helping me lug the vacuum around one or two days a week. And would you believe I never saw a bill? That's Phoebe for you. Why don't you fellas take off your coats and have a seat?"

"Thank you," Golden said.

We hung our coats from two hooks by the door and settled on the sofa. I reached down and stroked Lulu.

Katie took a slug from her can of Ballantine and said, "Phoebe deserved better than Junior, I don't care how many millions he had. I didn't blame her one bit when she filed for a divorce. He was a louse. Off on some grand adventure for months at a time, and when he came home, he cheated on her left, right, and sideways. Ask Bridget, who's all of nineteen. She can tell you. She'll be home in a minute. I just sent her to the corner to get me some Entenmann's doughnuts."

"You worked there for Phoebe three days a week?" Golden asked.

"That's right. Fifty dollars a day, cash. Bridget works as a cashier at our Duane Reade drugstore around the corner twenty hours a week. She shifted to weekends so she can help me at Phoebe's during the week. In case you're asking yourself, my husband, Bobby, took off for Florida with a barmaid at the Blarney Stone three years ago. But between the two of us, we get by okay. Plus, Phoebe, being the angel she is, has always given me steaks and pork chops from the freezer to take home and hand-me-down clothes for Bridget. She's much taller than Bridget, but they're both slim and I'm handy with a sewing machine."

"Have you had much contact with Siena Bing, the Realtor who's handling the sale of the house?" I asked.

Katie wrinkled her nose. "Much more than I care to. She's a snotty bitch. Right away, she told me the job I did on the kitchen floor wasn't up to her standards and that the bathrooms didn't sparkle like they should. She made it plain as day she wanted to get rid of me and hire a professional cleaning crew. I said to her, 'I work for Phoebe, not you, and unless Phoebe asks me to leave, I ain't going nowhere.' And she said to me, 'In that case, I need to have a conversation with her.'"

"And did she?" Golden asked.

"If she did, Phoebe didn't say a word to me about it."

"When was this?"

"The day before Junior's body was found."

"Phoebe's mother, Pippa, was there when we came to look at the house," I said.

"I didn't work that day, but no surprise there. As soon as Phoebe put the place up for sale, Pippa started butting in. She's a real piece of work. So superior, and nasty to boot. Didn't care one bit for the decorating job that Siena was doing and told her so. Pippa and Phoebe don't get along at all. But I can't imagine anyone gets along with that woman. She's just plain mean."

I heard footsteps out in the hallway. The door flew open, and in came a cute little blonde in a ponytail wearing a down jacket, jeans, and Adidas sneakers, clutching a box of chocolate doughnuts. "I got you your Entenmann's, Mom," she announced in a girlish voice, stiffening when she saw Golden and me seated there on the loveseat. "Who are these guys?"

Katie grabbed the doughnut box from her, tore it open, and began munching on one. "The dark-haired fellow is the police lieutenant investigating

Junior's murder. The tall one found Junior's body. He's married to Phoebe's cousin, Merilee Nash."

Bridget let out a gasp. "No lie?" Her face lit up excitedly. "And you have a basset hound puppy!" She fell to her knees and began making a fuss over her. "Hi, sweetie! Hi, cutie! You are so adorable. What's her name?"

"Lulu."

"What a doll you are, Lulu. Yes, you are. Yes, you are."

Lulu let out a low whoop, lapping up the attention.

Bridget knelt there next to her, petting her for a bit longer before she unzipped her jacket and tossed it aside. She wore a New York Jets sweatshirt under it. Despite her perky little butt, she had a tummy. If she'd been her mother's age, I would have attributed it to beer and doughnuts. Since she was nineteen, and Katie had a poisonous look on her face, I attributed it to something entirely different.

"Your mom said you've been helping her at the Singleton house ever since her hip started bothering her," said Golden, who'd noticed what I'd noticed.

"Yeah, I started about two months ago."

"Did you have much contact with Junior?"

Bridget reddened. "Now and then."

"What'd you think of him?"

"I thought he was dreamy. Tommy's been my boyfriend since I was fifteen, and we're going to get married because I love him, but I had such a huge crush on Junior."

Katie snorted. "Listen to her, will ya? She sounds like a teenager."

"Hello, I am a teenager, remember?"

"Tell them what he did to you. Go on, tell them."

Bridget's eyes widened. "You sure you want me to?"

"The lieutenant's investigating how Junior ended up on his dressing room floor with a steak knife in his eye," Katie said gruffly. "Somebody didn't think he was so dreamy. Tell them what happened. If you don't, I will."

"Well, okay . . ." Bridget said reluctantly. "A couple of months ago, when I was filling in for Mom, I was scrubbing a bathroom floor on my hands and knees, wearing jeans and a T-shirt. All of a sudden, I realized he was standing in the hall behind me. 'Sweet Jesus, your ass . . .' he said to me. I got all flustered and said, 'W-What about it?' He said, 'It's like two ripe peaches, that's what. I'm sorry, I must have you.' And the next thing I knew, my jeans were off, his pants were down, and he was inside of me right there on the bathroom floor. It all happened so fast I didn't have a chance to resist, not that I would have. I wanted him so bad I was ready for him before he even touched me."

"You little fool," Katie muttered angrily.

"He came right away. I guess he wanted me real bad, too." She reddened again. "I feel real funny talking about this to you guys."

"Please, don't," Golden said in a gentle voice. "It's important. Was that the only time that the two of you . . . ?"

"No, later that same day, when I was putting clean sheets on the bed in the master bedroom suite, there he was standing in the doorway saying, 'Damn, I cannot believe that ass. I've got to have you again. I've just got to.' And we went at it again with our pants down, except this time on the bed with a sheet under us that I was able to wash afterward."

"Was it what you dreamt it would be?" I asked.

Bridget frowned at me. "I don't know what you mean."

"Was it romantic?"

"Oh, I see. No, not at all. With Tommy, it's romantic. We get undressed. We hold each other. He's a big guy, a firefighter, but gentle and sweet. He tells me how much he loves me and kisses me a lot. Junior didn't kiss me at all."

"Was he wearing protection?"

Bridget gazed down at the floor. "No," she said faintly as her mother glared at her.

"So you're pregnant," Golden said.

She nodded.

"And how many weeks ago was this, Bridget?"

"My doctor says I'm eight weeks pregnant."

"That's fifty-six days—well before the exposure to infection stage."

"What infection?" Katie demanded.

"When the medical examiner performed the autopsy on Junior, he discovered that Junior was HIV positive. He had the AIDS virus. I don't believe he'd contracted it yet when he had unprotected sex with you, Bridget, but I'd still ask your doctor to test you just to be absolutely sure."

"Meanwhile," I said, "you're eight weeks pregnant with Junior's baby."

"Tommy's baby," Katie corrected me. "I told her to tell Tommy she was pregnant and that they have to get married right away. Which they're going to, next Saturday. As far as he knows, it's his baby."

"Doesn't Tommy wear a condom?" I asked Bridget.

"Yeah, but they're not a hundred percent perfect. My doctor said they can leak. Tommy proposed to me immediately. He's been wanting to get married, but he's twenty-two and thought maybe I was too young. We'll be getting married before I really start to show. I'll have a premature but healthy baby, and he'll never, ever know that he's not the father. Not unless one of you tells him."

"Your secret is safe with the two of us," I promised. Lulu let out a small yip. "Make that the three of us. Did you tell Junior you were pregnant?"

"I sure did."

"How did he take the news?"

"Calmly, like it wasn't the first time it had happened to him."

"Ya think?" Katie said sourly.

"He told me he knew a doctor in Locust Valley who ran a safe, sanitary clinic and that he'd make all of the arrangements and pay every penny. I told him I'm Catholic and don't believe in abortion, so he said he'd give me twenty-five thousand bucks to cover my medical bills and other expenses. It'd have to be in cash because he wanted to keep his name out of it. He also said you can't deposit ten thousand in your bank account without the bank reporting it to the IRS, so he gave me five envelopes with five thousand in each of them, all in hundred-dollar bills. Mom has deposited most of the first envelope in her account."

"Where are the other four?" Golden asked her.

"Under my mattress."

"May I see them?"

Bridget got up, went to her bedroom, and returned with them. The envelopes were plain and unmarked. Each was stuffed with crisp one-hundred-dollar bills. Golden gave them back to her, and she returned them to their hiding place.

"I don't really need the money that desperately," she said when she sat back down on the floor with Lulu. "Tommy is in the Firefighters Union and has good health insurance. Once we're married, I'll be covered by his plan, and so will the baby. But we'll be wanting to get our own place and buy a crib and furniture and stuff, so it'll come in plenty handy. I'll tell him Mom had saved it up and be careful about not spending too much of it at once. Mom can retire from cleaning and take care of the baby. I'll work full-time at the drugstore, and we'll all live happily ever after."

"I still think you should have held out for more money," Katie muttered. "The bastard raped you."

"He didn't rape me. How many times do I have to tell you? I wanted him as much as he wanted me. He was my fantasy love. But Tommy's my real-life love. He'll be a good husband and father."

"Junior was a no-good bastard," Katie shot back. "That's why Phoebe divorced him. She's a real lady. She deserved better."

"She gives me the creeps," Bridget confessed. "Nobody's that nice. Trust me, she's messed up."

Katie shook her head at her. "Half the words that come out of your mouth are total nonsense, you know that? Schoolgirl baloney."

Golden and I exchanged a nod. We were done. Time to leave this somewhat claustrophobic apartment. We climbed to our feet, put on our coats, thanked them for their time, and swore to them that we'd never tell a soul about the secret they'd shared with us.

Back out into the cold, windswept rain we went. The street was so deserted and quiet we could hear the pounding surf.

"Bridget's a nice enough kid," Golden said as we dashed through the rain back to his cruiser. Lulu climbed between us. "On the immature side, and not exactly a rocket scientist, but it seems as if it all worked out neatly for her, aside from the fact that the great love of her life is dead."

"Junior was strictly a schoolgirl fantasy. Tommy's the guy she was meant to marry. She got away lucky."

"Her old lady's a piece of work. But authentic. She is who she is. You don't meet many people like that, or at least I don't." He crinkled his nose, frowning at me. "Would you kindly explain something to me?"

"Happy to."

"Why does my car suddenly smell like castor oil?"

"Oh, that. Lulu is a shorthair with an oily coat. When it gets wet, it gives off an aroma."

"You're the word person, not me, but that's not an aroma. It's a stench. Is my seat going to smell like this forever?"

"That all depends."

"On what?"

"On whether or not you plan on keeping this car forever."

"I'm going to put in for a new one today."

"If I were you, I'd wait until you close this case. It rains a lot this time of year in the city. Mind you, it could be a lot worse. In the northern suburbs, the rain mixes with sleet, which is not only hell to drive in but turns into black ice overnight."

"You know what? You're reminding me of something very important."

"Which is . . . ?"

"Why I usually work alone." He started the car up, turned around, and headed back to the commercial district. "My stomach's growling. Feel like stopping for a sandwich?"

"Sure thing."

We found a takeout deli two blocks away that had a few tables inside, all of them empty. We ordered ham and cheese sandwiches and coffee from the scrawny old counterman, plus a tuna sandwich for Lulu, minus the bread. Then we sat down at a table.

"Katie Healey has a set of keys to the town house," Golden said after the counterman brought us our sandwiches and coffee and slid Lulu's tuna under the table. "She was in and out of the place regularly, loves Phoebe, and hated Junior even before the bastard knocked up her starry-eyed teenaged daughter." He took a ravenous bite of his sandwich. "She just became my prime suspect."

I went to work on my own sandwich. "Think she could have overpowered Junior with that steak knife?"

"I do. She would have had the element of surprise on her side. Plus, she's built like a tank."

"But why did she take two knives out of the box in the kitchen drawer?"

"I'll have to ask her that when I bring her in for questioning."

"And where is the second knife?"

"I'll have to ask her that, too," he said. "The medical examiner thinks Junior had been dead approximately eighteen hours when you found him on that dressing room floor." He glanced around as he wolfed down his sandwich. There was a phone booth in the corner of the deli. "I want to put a man to work tracing Katie's whereabouts at the time. Be right back."

Lulu and I finished eating while he made his call. "Did you enjoy that, little pard?"

She let out a yip in response.

Golden returned to our table a moment later with a troubled look on his face. Sat down heavily, reached for his container of coffee, and drank from it. Or tried to. He'd forgotten that he'd already finished it. "They've found the second steak knife that was missing from the wooden box," he said quietly.

"Oh yeah? Where is it?"

He raised his eyes to mine, his jaw muscles tightening. "In Mona Dale's left eyeball."

CHAPTER TWELVE

Mona was lying on her back on the cement floor of her basement studio in Hell's Kitchen with both eyes wide open. She looked shocked. Mona hadn't struck me as a woman who would be shocked by anything. She was wearing the same tank top and leggings she'd been wearing when I'd seen her the day before. Her bare feet still smelled.

There were two cruisers parked outside of her building along with a forensics van and the medical examiner's car. A dozen or more curious onlookers were standing around on the sidewalk. No camera crews. Word hadn't gotten out yet that the murder victim was the sexy, briefly famous lead singer of Four Hundred Blows. Once it did, the local TV news crews and tabloid army would descend en masse.

The heavyset medical examiner was kneeling next to her, taking her temperature. His assistant knelt nearby, attending to the contents of their medical bags. Two patrolmen were standing there with their hands on their hips, doing not much of anything.

Lulu crouched by the door. She gave me no indication of scent recognition. Whoever had tailed us there yesterday had not returned, entered the apartment, and killed Mona. If they had, Lulu would know. And make damned sure I knew.

"And so we meet again, Lieutenant," the medical examiner said gruffly.

"And so we do," Golden responded.

He glanced up at me. "You were at the Singleton house. You found Junior's body."

I nodded. "Stewart Hoag. I'm married to Merilee Nash. Her cousin, Phoebe, was Junior's ex-wife."

"Oh, right. What's the story with the dog?" he asked, glancing at Lulu.

"She's with me."

"Just make sure she doesn't compromise any evidence."

"She won't."

He studied the thermometer before he handed it to his assistant, who put it in a slender glass bottle of disinfectant with a screw-top lid, bagged it, tagged it, and placed it in one of their cases.

"How long's she been dead, Bob?" Golden asked.

"Since last evening, judging by her body temperature. Although this cement floor is damned cold, so I'm ballparking it. I can't give you a more precise time frame until I get her back to the lab."

"Who found her?"

"A DMV coworker," one of the patrolmen answered. "She said that Mona didn't show up for work this morning or answer her phone. So, on her lunch break, the coworker took a cab down here and buzzed her. When there was no answer, the super unlocked it, let her in, and they found the body."

"This building has a super?" Golden asked in surprise.

"I found that kind of amazing, too," the medical examiner said.

"Who'd want to kill her?" Golden asked me.

"Anyone who's had to wait in line for three hours at the DMV," one of the patrolmen cracked.

"Go wait outside," Golden ordered him. "I've got no use for a comedian right now."

He went slinking out the door, red-faced.

"Ordinarily," I replied, "I'd say someone from out of her past. An old bandmate with a grudge. Or possibly an obsessed fan. Emotions ran high in those days. So did the drug usage. Except that the missing Claude Dozorme steak knife in her eyeball narrows it down to the same person who killed Junior, doesn't it?"

"Agreed. Who knew about his relationship with Mona?"

"Jon Porterfield, his British investment broker pal, was the one who told me about the two of them. I don't think anyone else knew—except, that is, for whoever it was who followed me here yesterday when I left the phone book center in Grand Central. Mona asked me to bring her a six-pack of Pabst. Lulu picked up a familiar scent when we came out of the bodega around the corner and let me know about it. But you'll notice how calm she is right now. So whoever it was who tailed me here didn't enter this apartment. The killer has to be someone else."

The medical examiner looked up at me dubiously. "Are you telling me you take your cues from a puppy?"

"Lulu's no ordinary puppy. She's a world-class scent hound." To Golden, I said, "Mona did mention to me that Junior was trying to get out of a relationship with a clingy woman. Possibly more than just clingy. Possibly homicidal as well, and she punished Mona the same way she punished Junior."

Golden mulled that over. "Got anyone in mind?"

"Siena Bing."

"Does she strike you as the clingy type?"

"She strikes me as the driven, greedy, desperately lonely type. She also lied to me about getting tested for the virus."

Golden considered this for a moment before he said, "Is it just me or did it strike you as odd when Bridget Healey told us that Phoebe has always given her the creeps. Maybe there's a pissed off woman underneath that genteel exterior."

"It's not out of the question. I don't know her real well. I met Merilee three months ago, and have only seen Phoebe a handful of times. She seems like a nice person. Smart, sensitive. I like her. But if there's one thing I've learned so far in my life, it's that no one is who they appear to be."

"How about her eye doctor boyfriend, Barry Zallinger?"

"Ex-boyfriend. She just dumped him."

"How come?"

"He wimped out on her. Balked at the idea of her moving in with him. Told her he was concerned he'd get drawn into all of the tabloid attention Junior's murder is getting and that his patients wouldn't like it. They expect confidentiality. All of which sounded like bullshit to me. And, more significantly, to Phoebe."

"What a dick."

"My sentiments exactly. Her taste in men is not Phoebe's forte."

The medical examiner sat back on his heels, shaking his head. "Speaking of taste, it's hard to believe that the great Junior Singleton chose to spend his time in this dump with a tramp who needed to take a bath. I guarantee you her blood work will tell us she was HIV positive."

"And I guarantee you it won't," I said.

"I love it when guys walk in off the street and tell me my business," he groused.

"Care to place a wager on it, Fatso?"

He stuck his multiple chins out at me. "Who are you calling Fatso?"

"See anyone else in this apartment who's forty pounds overweight?"

"Fuck off."

Lulu immediately snarled and bared her puppy teeth at him.

"It's okay, girl. If he lays a single fat finger on me, he'll lose his job and have to go to work embalming cadavers in the basement of a mortuary in the Bronx."

"Like I said, fuck off. And while you're at it, clear the room and take your damned dog with you so the forensics team can get to work."

Lulu and I followed Golden out the door and up the stairs from the basement to the street. The rain had let up. I glanced at Grandfather's Benrus. It was 2:45.

"Real nice people you work with," I said to him.

"He's under a lot of pressure, same as I am."

"Where are you headed now?"

"To interview Jon Porterfield, who seems to be smack dab in the middle of this. Junior did wreck his marital plans, so he had a grudge against him."

"He swore to me he didn't."

"And you believed him?"

"Not exactly."

"He also steered you to Strutters' Walk and seems to be the only person who knew about Junior and Mona."

"Right," I agreed. "Unless someone else did."

"Like who?"

"No idea."

"Take a guess."

"I never guess."

He glared at me. I was getting on his nerves. "After that, I want to pay a call on Siena Bing, who is back to being my prime suspect—unless I'm missing something huge here. Which has been known to happen." He started toward his cruiser. When Lulu and I stayed put on the sidewalk, he frowned at me. "You're not coming along for the ride?"

"Correct. I've already gotten plenty from Jon. It's your turn. And I have no interest in speaking to Siena. She lied to me. I only talk to liars once."

"That must be nice. I wish I had a job like yours. So where are you headed?"

"I need to do some research for my SHE article. And then, at Merilee's request, I have to get home and keep Phoebe company. Merilee's been spending the day in a story conference with Robert Altman and Elliott Gould, and she said it'll probably continue on into the evening at Elaine's. That means Phoebe will be alone for hours and hours, which Merilee thinks might not be a healthy thing. She's on the fragile side right now." All of which was true, but wasn't the whole truth and nothing but the truth. I had a lead I wanted to follow up on by myself.

"Sure, okay. Can I drop you anywhere?"

"No, thanks. You're not going to miss us, are you?"

"Keep right on dreaming."

Lulu immediately started whimpering.

"Why is she doing that?" he wanted to know.

"Because you hurt her feelings."

"Oh, for Crissakes, Hoagy. Dogs don't have feelings."

"We're going to pretend we didn't hear that."

◆

Lulu and I walked our way east to Tenth Avenue, then strolled down toward Forty-Second Street. I stopped at a Citibank branch and withdrew $300 in cash because the place I was headed didn't take credit cards or checks. Then we made our way east on Forty-Second Street to one of my favorite stores in Times Square. I loved Times Square, home to strip clubs, X-rated movie houses, Sonny Chiba martial arts triple bills, dirty bookstores, dive bars, mystery meat steak houses, and some of the most wonderful stores to be found anywhere. There was the joke shop, which sold everything from plastic vomit to Richard Nixon masks. There was the newspaper store, which carried the daily papers of every major city in America. I'll confess I haunted it regularly when my novel came out to see what sort of reviews I was getting in papers like the *Washington Post* and the *Los Angeles Times.*

And there was my destination—the magazine store, a gold mine of research material that had an amazing supply of magazines you couldn't find anywhere else. It stocked back issues of everything from *Life, Look,* and *Cracked* to the *Saturday Evening Post, Collier's,* and countless others that no longer existed, dating all the way back to the 1940s, as well as recent issues of weeklies and monthlies that were still very much with us. It also had a generous back-room supply of *Playboy* dating back to its origins in the 1950s, as well as cheesy pre-Hef porn mags, if that's what you were looking for.

I knew exactly what I was looking for—every issue for the past five years of one of America's most popular slick monthlies. Sixty magazines in all. I gathered them up in my arms and plopped them down on the counter. Two gaunt, pale old guys ran the place. After I'd shelled out $180, plus tax, they stuffed them in two plain brown paper bags, double thickness for strength. From there, Lulu and I strode due west to the main branch of the New York Public Library on Forty-Second Street and Fifth Avenue.

I parked myself in the vast reading room with my supply of magazines before me as Lulu curled up on my feet, and I started working my way backward from the previous month's issue. Fortunately, the table of contents was easy to find and very thorough, which made for quick work. But I had to make it through eighteen months' worth of issues before I hit pay dirt. Stared at it. Stared at it some more, my pulse quickening. I tucked that issue in my soft briefcase, re-bagged the rest, and toted them back to the magazine store, where they bought back what they'd just sold me for twenty-five cents on the dollar, which was their standard procedure. Once a struggling cash-strapped author, always a struggling cash-strapped author.

Then I caught a cab, and Lulu and I headed home, my head spinning as a whole new set of pieces began falling into place.

And the day was still young.

CHAPTER THIRTEEN

The tabloid news horde had vacated Charlton Street, no doubt for Mona's place in Hell's Kitchen. The relative calm was most welcome. I heard the sounds of a violin coming from the living room when I walked in the door shortly after five o'clock. Phoebe was playing Bartók's String Quartet no. 4, which was the piece her former chamber music quartet had been working on before Barry caused a serious rupture in the quartet by being a two-timing scumbag. Phoebe was not a supremely gifted violinist, but she'd taken lessons for years, was diligent, and loved to play the instrument, which is what mattered the most. And she had plenty of emotion in her vibrato that day, possibly because she had a lot of emotion boiling inside of her.

When Lulu ambled in to say hello and possibly get a belly rub, she stopped playing. I followed Lulu in there, though I had no expectations of a belly rub.

"Oh, hi, Hoagy," she said a bit shyly, standing there in a Brearley sweatshirt with the sleeves cut off, jeans, and thick wool socks. Her long blond hair was tied back in a ponytail. A fire was crackling in the fireplace. "I hope you don't mind me practicing down here. It got cold up on the fourth floor, and I can't wear anything bulky when I'm playing. I need my arms free."

"Of course not, Phoebe. Our house is your house. I'm just going to run upstairs and change. Be right back." As soon as I got upstairs, I slid that precious magazine I'd found into the top drawer of my desk. Then I hung up my tweed herringbone jacket and charcoal flannel slacks and put on an old pair of jeans with the navy blue cashmere turtleneck I'd been wearing. By the time I returned downstairs, Phoebe had tucked her violin in its case and was seated on the sofa before the fire. She'd put one of Merilee's well-worn flannel shirts, which is to say one of my well-worn flannel shirts, on over her bare-armed sweatshirt and was in the process of liberating her lovely blonde hair from its ponytail, running her fingers through it so it draped over her shoulders.

"Would you like a glass of Chianti Classico?"

She smiled at me faintly. "I would love a glass of Chianti Classico."

I poured two glasses in the kitchen, returned with them, and sat on the sofa with her. We clinked glasses.

"And how has your day been?" I asked her after we each took sips.

"I stopped off at Brearley to clear out my things and inform the school administrators that my relationship with them was officially over. They were shocked, possibly even apoplectic, and assured me that my suspension was strictly temporary, just until things quieted down. I said, 'You have known me since I was a student here. Either you have faith in me or you don't, and since you clearly don't, I no longer wish to be associated with you.'"

"Good for you, Phoebe," I said.

"I must admit I was kind of proud of myself," she confessed, coloring slightly. "Then I gave goodbye hugs to the teachers who'd been my friends there, returned here, and dusted and scoured this place from top to bottom."

"I thought it seemed different in here. It's missing that protective coating of Charlton Street soot."

Lulu moseyed in and curled up in Phoebe's lap contentedly.

"Did you and Lieutenant Golden learn anything new about Junior's case?"

"There were quite a few developments, actually. Just for starters, Katie Healey's daughter, Bridget, is eight weeks pregnant with Junior's baby."

Her blue eyes widened. "You have got to be kidding."

"I wish I were."

"Why, that son of a bitch," she said angrily.

"Bridget's a not-too-bright kid who thought Junior was dreamy, and he took advantage of her infatuation one day when they were alone together in the house."

"Leave this to me," she said with cold-eyed disapproval. "I'll take care of everything."

"No need, it's already taken care of. Bridget's marrying her fiancé, Tommy the firefighter, on Saturday. He believes, and will always believe, that their somewhat premature baby is his. Tommy gets good health insurance through the Firefighters Union, so they'll be fine when it comes to medical expenses. Junior did offer to pay for an abortion, but Bridget's a Catholic, so that was off the table. He gave her twenty-five thousand dollars in cash instead for the medical expenses she'll accrue and to furnish the nursery in their new apartment, which will be in the same Rockaway Beach neighborhood where everyone they know lives. Bridget will work full-time at the drugstore where she now works part-time. Grandma Katie will babysit, watch Bette Davis movies on TV, and no longer have to lug around a vacuum cleaner."

"But what about Junior's HIV-positive status?"

"Golden did warn her about it, but she hasn't felt ill, and after eight weeks, something like 97 percent of the people who've been exposed to the virus show symptoms. So it's likely that she had sex with him before he was exposed to the virus himself. But the lieutenant did urge her to get a blood test."

Phoebe finished off her wine, clearly shaken. "Unbelievable . . ."

"Hang on, I'm just getting warmed up." I fetched the wine bottle from the kitchen, refilled both of our glasses, and sat back down. "They found your missing steak knife."

"They did? Where was it?"

"In Mona Dale's left eyeball. Her body was on the floor of her apartment."

Phoebe looked at me blankly. "Who is Mona Dale?"

"Her name doesn't mean anything to you?"

"No. Should it?"

"She was a pretty big punk rock star for a while. Major sex symbol, almost as big as Debbie Harry, the lead singer of Blondie."

"Punk was never my thing," Phoebe said with a shrug.

"I'm not surprised. But it was Junior's, and he'd been seeing Mona romantically for a while. In fact, they were deeply involved. I don't mean to bring this up to hurt you."

"Believe me, you're not. I stopped caring about who he was involved with ages ago. I'm sorry that someone murdered him, but my emotional involvement is nil, so don't worry about sparing my feelings. Where did this Mona person live?"

"In a dark, dingy tenement basement studio in Hell's Kitchen."

"My God, this is getting weird," she said with a shake of her head.

"No, it started out weird. Now it's getting scary."

"Does Lieutenant Golden have any idea who killed her?"

"The same person who killed Junior, since the murder weapon was the second steak knife from the box in your kitchen drawer. Beyond that? No, other than that it would appear to be someone who has a set of keys to your house, since the forensics team found no signs of forced entry. We drove out to Rockaway Beach together this morning to talk to Katie and Bridget. I was with him when he phoned in and found out about Mona. We hightailed it to her place. When we split up, he was on his way to interview your Realtor, Siena, who was another of Junior's conquests and is not home sick with the flu. She had unprotected sex with Junior, is HIV positive, and has known about it for two weeks. My sense is that the lieutenant considers her a prime suspect. She certainly had a good reason to be pissed off at Junior. As to why she'd want to kill Mona, too, maybe the lieutenant picked up something when he interviewed her. I haven't spoken to him yet."

"My goodness, your day has certainly been eventful."

"It wasn't dull. And Lulu loves police work, don't you, girl?"

She let out a low whoop, her tail thumping.

The phone rang in the kitchen. I got up and went in there. It was my line that was blinking. I picked it up, hoping it was Merilee.

It wasn't.

"Hiya, Chief," I said.

"Chief? Why are you calling me Chief?" Pippa Longworth demanded.

"Because I'm writing an article for you. I always call my editor Chief."

As soon as Phoebe heard me say the words "article" and "editor," she quickly got up off the sofa, took out her violin, and resumed playing Bartók, good and loud.

Pippa said, "Let's get something straight, Stewart. You're not Clark Kent, and I'm not Perry White."

"Damn, and here I thought we were going to have fun working together."

"I do believe I can hear Phoebe practicing."

"Yes, she's working on a Bartók piece in the living room."

"She hates it when I disturb her, so I won't. I was simply calling to assure her she can always move back in with me now that Meredith has given her the boot. As has Brearley, I understand."

"You certainly have good sources. Phoebe told me they'd suspended her until things, quote-unquote, quiet down, at which time they can discuss her future. She said that since they clearly have no faith in her, there was nothing to discuss, and quit her job on the spot. It was a very polite fuck-you."

"She's always been very polite. Seriously, Hoagy, she should be home with me at a time like this. There's no substitute for family."

"Merilee is family."

Pippa immediately shifted gears. "How is the article coming along?"

"I'd prefer to show it to you when I have a completed draft, not give it to you in dribbles over the phone."

"Will you at least tell me if you saw Lieutenant Golden today?"

"I did."

"Tell me, what's the story with his love life?"

"He's not available."

"Don't kid yourself. Everyone is available."

"You sound awfully interested in him."

"Sure I am. He's going places in the department and he's a hunk. His wardrobe is atrocious, but that's an easy fix. He's age appropriate, almost, and I'm lonely. Men who are over thirty-five want a lovely young prize like Phoebe, not an aging frump like me."

"Oh, please. You don't even look forty."

"May I say hello to Merilee?"

"I'm afraid she's not here. She's meeting with Robert Altman and Elliott Gould straight through the evening."

"Sounds fascinating. Give her my best." And with that, she hung up.

As soon as I returned to the living room, Phoebe put her violin back in its case, sat back down on the sofa, and said, "What did Mother want?"

"To tell you that since you're no longer rooming with Meredith, she thinks you should move in with her."

"That'll be the day."

"You sounded just like John Wayne in *The Searchers* when you said that. Gosh, you're tough."

She let out a laugh, which made her eyes widen in surprise. "I swear that's the first time I've laughed in I don't know how long."

"For some reason, I seem to have that effect on people. About your living situation . . . "

"What about it?"

"As far as Merilee and I are concerned, you can stay here for as long as you want, now that moving in with Barry is a definite Never Gonna Happen."

"The idea of me so much as speaking to Barry again is a definite Never Gonna Happen."

"But I do have an idea that's either incredibly brilliant or really stupid—my fifth-floor walk-up on West Ninety-Third. I'm still paying rent on it, but I live here now, so it's just sitting there unoccupied. If you don't mind living in an unheated dump in a crummy neighborhood while you're figuring out what you want to do next, it's all yours."

Her pale blue eyes brightened. "That's such a kind offer, Hoagy. When you say it's unheated . . ."

"The building has heat, but almost none of it makes it all the way up to the fifth floor. And what little does is sucked out of the skylights in the kitchen and bathroom."

"It has skylights? Goodness, it sounds like an artist's loft."

"Writer's loft. That's where I wrote my novel. I was twenty-four and broke when I rented it for the princely sum of $225 a month. I do have a couple of space heaters, and it's clean. Well, it might be a bit dusty right now since I only stop by to get my mail. It's yours if you want it, but if you'd rather stay here with us, we're happy to have you."

Phoebe considered it for a moment. "I must say, it sounds weirdly tempting. I'd be able to collect my thoughts in peace and practice my violin to my heart's content. Do you have a stereo?"

I nodded. "A good one, complete with a turntable, so you can play vinyl. If you'd like, we could go take a look at it."

"What, do you mean right now?"

"Why not? Merilee's tied up all evening. I'll even take you to Tony's for dinner afterward. It's my favorite neighborhood Italian restaurant. Lulu's, too."

Lulu confirmed that with a low whoop. She loved Tony's fried calamari.

"Hoagy, you've got yourself a deal," Phoebe said with a burst of enthusiasm. "Just let me put on some presentable clothes."

"Make sure they're warm ones."

"Is the apartment that cold?"

"No, but our Jaguar ragtop is. It's been sitting in the garage around the corner for days and could use a workout. Unless, that is, you'd rather take a cab."

"Absolutely not."

I gave Lulu an anchovy while we waited for Phoebe to change clothes. I left a note on the kitchen table for Merilee in case she got home before we did. Phoebe came back down a few minutes later dressed in a cream-colored four-ply-cashmere shawl cardigan, gabardine slacks, and boots. I helped her on with her coat, put my wool-lined trench coat and fedora back on, and we set off down Charlton with Lulu.

Walking with Phoebe was like walking with a slimmed-down version of Merilee with a slightly shorter stride. She'd brushed out her long blond hair so it shone in the streetlights. Her face glowed with anticipation. She truly was a lovely woman. Quite a catch for the right guy.

Rocco was in his cubicle when we got to the garage. He grinned at me and said, "How are ya, Mr. H? And who do we have here?" he asked admiringly. "Don't tell me you're stepping out on Merilee. You've got a definite type, I'll say that for you. Blond and beautiful. She even looks a little bit like Merilee."

"That's because she's her cousin, Phoebe. Phoebe, say hello to Rocco."

"Hello to Rocco," she complied obediently.

He let out a guffaw. "I can tell she's been spending time with you, Mr. H. You got a husband, Phoebe?"

"I'm divorced."

"Whattaya do for a living?"

"I was teaching at Brearley, but I've just quit."

"I'm looking for a bookkeeper if you get desperate. I'll go fetch the Jag. I've been running the battery so it won't die." He strode up the ramp to the second floor, and a moment later, I heard him start it up with a throaty roar. Then he eased it down the ramp, pulled up beside us, put on the parking brake, and climbed out, letting it idle. "I turned on the heat, so to speak."

Phoebe gazed at our red 1958 Jaguar XK150 with its sixty-spoke wire wheels in awe. "My God, it's gorgeous."

"That's right, you've never seen it. When Merilee and I first met, she told me she'd always wanted a vintage British ragtop, so I bought her one."

"I've never been in an antique sports car before."

"In that case, prepare to have some fun."

She got in a bit gingerly. "My God, these seats are leather," she said as Lulu wasted no time getting comfy on her lap.

I thanked Rocco, waved goodbye, and tore out of there to Hudson, then took Fourteenth Street to Eighth Avenue and sped uptown, shifting gears as I zipped my way through the traffic past the columned grandeur of the McKim, Mead & White James A. Farley Post Office building, followed by the consummate ugliness of the Port Authority Bus Terminal. Eighth Avenue merged with Broadway at Columbus Circle, and soon we were on the Upper West Side.

"Phoebe, may I ask you a nosy question?"

"I'm enjoying this ride so much you can ask me anything."

"Did you love Junior?"

She hesitated. "I loved the idea of him, but I scarcely saw him. He was always gallivanting around the world, and when we were together, we weren't that intimate in terms of sharing our feelings. He didn't talk about himself much or confide in me. He was . . . secretive. And our sex life was not the least bit satisfying. At least not for me. Actually, I think Mother was more thrilled that I was married to him than I was, because of his wealth and social cachet. She pushed me hard to encourage him when he showed an interest in me. Not that I've ever understood why he did."

"You're a beautiful woman, Phoebe."

"Says the man who's married to a glamorous film star." She glanced over at me. "You're not a five-minute man, are you?"

"You don't really expect me to answer that, do you?"

"No, I was just teasing you. I guess I'm not very good at it."

"You're doing fine."

"Do you really mean that?"

"I wouldn't have said it if I didn't."

By then, we'd made it to West Eighty-Sixth Street. Sloan's supermarket was still doing a brisk after-work business, so the girls weren't out yet on Strutters' Walk. I made a left at West Ninety-Third and crossed West End Avenue, which was lined with prewar high-rise buildings, then eased my way past what had once been fine town houses. These days, they were broken up into eight or ten small one-bedroom apartments. Some were well kept up. Some, like mine, were not.

I found a parking space not too far away, got out, locked my door, walked around the car, and opened Phoebe's door so I could lift Lulu out of her lap. After I'd set Lulu down on the sidewalk, I took Phoebe's slender hand and helped her out, locked her door, and led her into the vestibule of my building, which smelled of body odor and urine because a homeless man often slept there. I had some junk mail and a Con Ed bill. Alberta had rerouted my business correspondence and royalty checks to the Charlton Street house.

I unlocked the front door, and we started our way upstairs, hearing the authentic sounds of New York City's dreamers as we climbed. The aspiring Broadway musical tap dancer who lived on the first floor. The folk singer/acoustic guitarist who lived on the second floor. The young actor who lived on the third floor was rehearsing a scene from *A Streetcar Named Desire* with a young actress. The opera singer who lived below me was doing her voice exercises. Everyone who has a dream comes to the city to make it a reality. Very, very few succeed. It never failed to amaze me that I had.

Lulu, who'd walked a lot that day, started having a hard time with the stairs by the time we reached the third floor. I picked her up and carried her the rest of the way. At thirty-two pounds, she was getting to be a bit of an armload. When we arrived at the fifth floor, I unlocked the door, flicked on the hall light, and ushered Phoebe inside, where it was the same temperature as the unheated hallway.

I turned on the kitchen light and my green-shaded desk lamp and cranked up the electric space heaters.

"It faces the rear, so you don't hear much street noise," I said as I led her into the living room, which had room enough for my desk, a corduroy loveseat, a good leather chair, and my floor-to-ceiling brick and board bookcases. The well-worn parquet floor was evidence that this had once been a very nice house. An old Afghan rug I'd found covered much of it.

"So this is where you wrote your novel?" Phoebe asked me as she gazed around. I couldn't tell if she was awestruck or horrified.

"Indeed. Sometimes I'd have the manuscript spread out all over the floor and would scribble notes on it on my hands and knees. I notice you haven't taken your coat off. Are you cold or too bashful to show off your cleavage?"

She giggled. "You're a very silly man. Has anyone ever told you that?"

"Pretty much everyone has, actually." I led her into the kitchen, with its skylight soaring overhead. "There isn't enough room in here for a table, so I used to eat at my desk or standing over the sink, which is a time-honored bachelor tradition." There was a small refrigerator, a four-burner gas stove, only three of which worked, and an overhead oven that had never worked at all.

I put down some water for Lulu, who'd worked up a thirst climbing the stairs, and ushered Phoebe into the bedroom, which had enough room for a double bed, a nightstand, and a 1940s dresser I'd bought at a used furniture place on Amsterdam Avenue for twelve dollars. I turned on the nightstand lamp and gazed up at the ceiling over the bed. I had memorized every crack in that ceiling after staring at it night and day for three years while I was writing my book.

"Moving right along on our tour, the bathroom is this way." I led her down the tiny hallway and turned on the light. "It's got a combination shower tub, as you can see, a highly desirable turquoise and pink tile floor, another skylight to let the heat out while you shower, and an ancient sink with separate hot and cold faucets. No mixer. You have to fill the sink to make your own warm water. You don't see too many of these anymore."

She gazed up at the skylight, then back at me. Again, I couldn't tell if she was awestruck or horrified.

"I couldn't afford high-quality space heaters before, but I could get you a couple now so that you won't feel as if you're living in Lara's apartment in *Doctor Zhivago*. It's a dump, no two ways about it, but if you want to be by yourself for a few weeks while you sort things out, then this is the place. You can play your violin to your heart's content and rest assured that absolutely no one will drop in on you. It might be just what you need. Think about it," I said, heading back into the living room, where Lulu was snoring softly in the leather chair.

"I don't have to think about it," Phoebe declared. "I love it."

I looked at her in surprise. "You do?"

"I do. It's totally real. Plus, it makes me feel closer to you."

"And that matters because . . . ?"

"I have a huge crush on you, don't you know that?"

"I'm very fond of you, too. But Merilee and I just got married, remember? You were there. Saw it happen in living color."

"I know, I know . . ." She lowered her gaze, blushing. "I shouldn't have blurted that out, but it's the truth. I don't seem to have very good luck with men. You're the only one I've ever met who's actually who he appears to be. You're not a fraud. You're not cruel. You're kind, funny, talented . . ."

"Careful, my head swells to fit any occasion."

"Can I move in here tomorrow? I don't have a lot of stuff. Just a couple of suitcases, my violin, music stand, and books. I'm something of a vagabond these days. Not to mention a lonely, unemployed train wreck."

"Beg to differ. I think you're terrific. And some lucky guy is going to find that out before you know it. Tomorrow will be fine. Shall we shake on it?"

"Could we hug instead?"

"Why not?"

I took her in my arms. She was only an inch or two shorter than Merilee, but her shoulders were so much narrower she felt fragile. I hugged her gently. She hugged me tightly and showed no interest in letting go. Just held on to me, sighing contentedly. It was totally nonsexual, or at least it was until she plastered her pelvis against mine. I pulled away and planted a gentle kiss on her forehead, which proved to be a tactical error. She raised her face to mine, her pale blue eyes huge and inviting, and kissed me on the mouth, sliding her tongue between my lips in eager search of mine.

I backed away from her before I let things go any further, which for damned sure was not going to happen. What was it that Bridget Healey had said about her? "She gives me the creeps. Nobody's that nice. Trust me, she's messed up."

Possibly, airheaded nineteen-year-old Bridget was right. Possibly, Phoebe was out of her fucking mind. Hell, possibly, it was she who'd murdered her ex-husband and Mona. At this point, I wasn't ruling out anything.

"I'm sorry," she said in a husky voice. "I shouldn't have done that."

"It's okay."

"No, it's not. It's just that I'm so terrified. I have no husband, no job, and-and how do I know I'm not going to be the next victim?"

"Lieutenant Golden won't let anything happen to you. Besides, if you were going to be the next victim, we'd know."

"How on earth would you know?"

"Because there'd be a third knife missing."

"Oh . . . that's true."

"Ready for some dinner?"

"That would be great," she said, smiling at me.

"I'll give you a set of keys in the morning, and we'll move your stuff in—if you still feel the same way tomorrow, that is."

"Oh, I will, Hoagy. There isn't a doubt in my mind."

◆

I didn't have to worry about being bombarded by Michael Jackson singing "Thriller" when we strolled into Tony's, which was strictly a Sinatra establishment. For me, Tony's was like the Blue Mill. It gave me an inkling of what it must have been like to live in New York in the 1940s.

Tony came to the door to welcome us with his arms open wide. "Hoagy, where have you been? You brought the gorgeous movie star Miss Merilee Nash here back in October, then I don't see you again."

"Strictly because I moved in with her downtown on Charlton Street, which may have been a mistake because I miss coming here. And Lulu misses your calamari." She let out a yip, her tail thumping.

"She is getting to be such a big girl," he said, bending down to pet her.

"Yes, she is. The good news is that we're going to be moving soon. I'm hoping it'll be walking distance away on Central Park West."

"This would make me very happy." Tony gazed appreciatively at Phoebe. "But who is this gorgeous creature?"

"Say hello to Merilee's cousin Phoebe. She's planning to take over my old apartment. Once she tastes your food, you'll be seeing a lot of her."

"I hope so. Welcome, Phoebe. You're as beautiful as Merilee. Tell me, Hoagy, how did you choose which one to marry?"

"It was simple. I met Merilee first."

He let out a roar of laughter.

"I love your place," Phoebe said to him as he led us to a table. Sinatra was serenading us with "Fly Me to the Moon." "It feels so homey."

"You must visit us often," he said to her. "I know Lulu will want fried calamari, and Hoagy will want our homemade sausages, linguine in olive oil and garlic, and a side order of sautéed spinach. Would you like to see a menu?"

"Not necessary. I'll have veal piccata, please, with a bit of pasta in olive oil and garlic. And I'd love some sautéed spinach, too."

"Excellent," he said, beaming at her approvingly. He disappeared into the kitchen to place our order, then returned with a bottle of my favorite Chianti Classico, which he uncorked at the table. He poured a bit into my glass to taste. On my enthusiastic nod, he filled both of our glasses and went off to greet the couple who had just come in the door.

We clinked glasses and sipped our wine, her eyes shining at me.

"Did you ever wonder?" she asked.

"Wonder what?"

"What would have happened if I was the one you'd met first?"

She gives me the creeps. Nobody's that nice. Trust me, she's messed up.

"I don't have to wonder," I said, sipping my wine. "Allow me to tell you a little story. After my book really took off, the *New Yorker* assigned its most highly regarded young reporter to do a profile of me. She spent three days and nights with me, not only grilling me with a million incredibly smart, tough questions but hitting my old punk hangouts with me and my favorite after-hours clubs in Spanish Harlem, throwing back tequila, shot for shot. Her name was Jillian. She had a mane of flaming red hair, was gorgeous, talented, smart, and funny. I was absolutely crazy about her. As soon as she turned in the story, we jumped into bed together and didn't come up for air. We were the hottest young couple in New York media circles until something unexpected happened."

Phoebe studied me curiously over her wine glass. "Which was . . . ?"

"I had dinner one night at the Blue Mill on Commerce Street with my college chum, Ezra Spooner.

He's the fellow who stood up for me at our wedding at city hall."

"Oh, sure. Of course."

"Anyhow, as Ez and I were heading to our table, he stopped to say hi to a fellow he knew, an agent, who was having dinner with Merilee. She stared at me. I stared at her. And we kept on staring. It was pure magic. We ended up in bed together that night, and the next morning, she invited me to move in. I did, and we've been fused together ever since. Nothing like the instant chemistry that Merilee and I have together had ever happened to me before. At least three weeks had gone by before I realized I hadn't explained to Jillian why I'd totally disappeared and hadn't returned any of her calls. I'm not a perfect guy, believe me. So the answer to your question about what might have happened if you were the one I'd met first is—"

"That's okay." Phoebe gazed across the table at me despondently as Tony brought us a platter of antipasto and a basket of bread. "You answered it."

CHAPTER FOURTEEN

After we dropped the Jag off with Rocco, we strolled back to the Charlton house. Since it was nearly ten o'clock, this qualified as Lulu's bedtime walk, and she had numerous stops to make. When we got home, the lights were on in the living room, meaning Merilee was home from dinner at Elaine's with Robert Altman and Elliott Gould.

Before we went inside, Phoebe put her hand on my arm and said, "Thanks, Hoagy," her voice quavering slightly.

"For what?"

"For the loan of your apartment. For dinner. For being such a good guy."

"You will get through this, you know. My guess? In about a month, the administrators at Brearley will be begging you on their hands and knees to come back. Also that you're going to meet someone great. You're quite a catch."

"Would you do me a huge favor?"

"Name it."

"Can I have one more hug?"

"Hugs are always available."

She slid into my arms and clutched me tightly before she released me. I unlocked the door and we went inside, hanging our winter coats on the hooks in the vestibule. There was no sign of Merilee downstairs. When I called out her name, I heard a muffled response from the second floor. I went up there and discovered she was taking a bubble bath. Phoebe called out good night to her, smiling at me wistfully from the hallway before she headed up to the guest room. I went back downstairs to top off Lulu's water bowl and turn out the lights. Then I carried her up to the master suite, closed the hallway door, and tapped on the bathroom door. "May we come in and say hello?"

"Please do."

It was like a steam bath in there, the huge tub filled with what had to be the hottest water Merilee could possibly tolerate. Lulu scampered into the room, yipping and yapping since she hadn't seen her mommy all day. Merilee reached a soapy arm out of the tub and stroked her. "Yes, sweetness. I've missed you, too."

Her hair was up in a bun, her face flushed. She looked exhausted. "Don't mind me, darling, I'm just trying to sweat Robert Altman out of my pores."

I put a folded towel on the floor for Lulu to curl up on and stripped down to my Buster Poindexter T-shirt and boxer shorts before I slumped in the makeup table chair, plenty exhausted myself. "It didn't go well with the three of you?"

"If, by 'the three of you,' you're referring to Elliott Gould, he wasn't with us, for the simple reason that he's in Los Angeles, and Robert didn't bother to make sure of that before he flew here to meet with us. He's the most disorganized, arrogant, obnoxious egomaniac I've ever met. The man oozes alcohol and rottenness to his core. He's made some very good movies. McCabe & Mrs. Miller is amazing. But I certainly don't want to work with him. He's a prick."

"Did you eat at Elaine's?"

"Where else? He wanted Liz Smith and Cindy Adams to know he was in town to meet with me about his latest project."

"Is the script any good?"

Merilee snorted. "There is no script. Scripts are for other, lesser filmmakers. What he has is a mental image."

"Of what?"

"A man and a woman floating on their backs in a swimming pool, holding hands. He's sure that if he gets Elliott and me in front of a camera together and we start improvising dialogue about our marriage that a film will magically emerge."

"Does he have a title for it?"

"*Floating,* what else? How was your day? Better than mine, I hope."

"I gather that while you were being held prisoner by Altman's alcohol-soaked genius, you didn't catch any of the news."

She immediately turned serious. "Why, what's happened?"

"They found that second steak knife—in Mona Dale's left eyeball."

She let out a gasp. "Oh my Lord, Hoagy."

"I was with Lieutenant Golden when he got the news, so Lulu and I ended up at the crime scene."

"Which was where?"

"Her dingy basement apartment in Hell's Kitchen."

"You . . . saw her?"

"I did."

She reached for my hand and squeezed it. "I'm so sorry, darling."

"That makes two of us." On Lulu's yip, I quickly added, "Three of us."

"Who would have wanted Mona dead?"

"Someone insanely jealous and vengeful. Junior had a clingy lover whom he was trying to break it off with. Mona told me so. We know he had a thing with Siena, who has keys to the house, access to the steak knives, and is HIV positive, thanks to him. Lieutenant Golden likes her for it."

"Do you?"

"She's certainly in play. Junior was not, by the way, having sex with Jill Perlo, the renowned climatologist, although it wasn't for lack of trying. I spoke to her this morning in Washington Square Park. I wanted to find out what they were arguing about at the Lunch Club last week. She told me he'd been so impressed by her visionary work that he'd provided Canterbury

College with what had to be millions of dollars of funding for her research after she became too outspoken and controversial for MIT Junior, being Junior, was more interested in her attractive bod than he was in her research. Jill happens to be a lesbian who's in a committed relationship. When he found that out, he pulled his funding for her computer research and even tried to deny her access to it."

Merilee shook her head in disgust. "What a prick."

"Is that your word for the day?"

"It seems to be."

"It's a good word, suitable for many reprehensible types. So Jill had a motive for killing him. What she didn't have was a reason to kill Mona."

Merilee took my hand and squeezed it. "I'm sorry you had such a horrid day, darling."

"Hang on, there's more. Golden and I drove out to Rock-Rock-Rockaway Beach to talk to Katie Healey, Phoebe's housekeeper, and her nineteen-year-old daughter, Bridget, who's been helping Katie part-time. Bridget is eight weeks pregnant, and guess who the father is—or I should say was."

Her green eyes widened. "Junior raped her?"

"Not exactly. She was madly in love with him in a dreamy, schoolgirl sort of way, even though she's engaged to her firefighter boyfriend, Tommy. One day, she was on her hands and knees scrubbing the bathroom floor. Junior appeared in the doorway, said her ass looked like two ripe peaches, and before you can say Reginald Martinez Jackson, her jeans were off and he was inside her right there on the bathroom floor."

"Let me guess. It was over in five minutes."

"If that long. And it happened again later that same day when she was changing the sheets on the bed. Both times were so sudden she didn't even think about protection, although she has no HIV symptoms, so it's likely that it happened before Junior got exposed to it by shooting up with Chantelle. But Bridget did get pregnant. Junior offered to pay for an abortion, but she's Catholic and doesn't believe in abortions, so she's rushing Tommy the firefighter to the altar before she gets too obvious a tummy. This Saturday, in fact. Tommy will go through life thinking thc baby is his. No one will ever know otherwise."

"Could Katie have killed Junior as payback?"

"Golden doesn't think so. She was home in Rockaway at the approximate time of his death, according to the men he's put on the case. And it's hard to imagine why either she or Bridget would want to kill Mona."

"Wow . . ." Merilee puffed out her flushed cheeks. "Were you able to spend some time with Phoebe?"

"Yes. She was playing the violin in the living room when I got home, and was horrified when I told her the missing steak knife had been located, although she claimed she wasn't familiar with Mona Dale or aware that Junior had been seeing her. Pippa phoned. She wants Phoebe to move in with her, which will never, ever happen. But that woman sure has sources. She not only knew that Meredith had kicked Phoebe out of her apartment but also that the administrators at Brearley had suspended her until this unseemly mess is cleared up. Phoebe told them that they either have faith in her or they don't, and since they obviously don't, she was resigning effective immediately."

"Good for her. It's nice to see her stand up for herself."

"I agree. I think Lulu's been an empowering influence on her. Except she now has no job and no place to live until she can go apartment hunting."

"I've told her she can stay here as long as she wants."

"I have, too, but she knows we're newlyweds and want our privacy. Just for the hell of it, I mentioned I still have my unheated fifth-floor walk-up on West Ninety-Third, complete with skylights, that's just sitting there vacant, and told her she's welcome to live there in total peace and quiet, playing her violin to her heart's content, until her life gets straightened out. The idea seemed to appeal to her, so we drove up there in the Jag. She looked the place over and pronounced it ideal. She intends to move in there tomorrow. I'll buy her a couple of new high-efficiency space heaters so she won't freeze."

Merilee considered it for a moment. "Maybe privacy is just what she needs right now. That was a brilliant suggestion, darling."

"But I should caution you—she told me that being there made her feel closer to me."

Merilee looked at me, puzzled. "Meaning?"

"Believe it or not, she seems to have developed a crush on me, so it's your responsibility, starting tomorrow, to disabuse her of the idea that I'm the perfect guy. I'm counting on you."

She arched an eyebrow at me. "I'll do my best. Did you manage to squeeze in any time to work on your article on Junior for Pippa?"

"I did. Jill Perlo had interesting insights into him, actually. Almost everyone in the world thought he led a dream life—climbing Everest, racing Formula One Ferraris, Alpine downhill skiing, and so on. She didn't. She thought he was an unsettled, deeply unhappy man who had a death wish. I happen to agree with her. Let's face it, anyone these days who shares a needle with a street hooker has to have a death wish. It's almost as if he wanted to give himself AIDS."

Merilee considered this for a moment before she said, "That won't exactly fit with Pippa's image of Junior as America's last gentleman hero."

"If she wants a puff piece, then she picked the wrong boy. I'm going to write it the way I see it, and if Pippa doesn't like it, Alberta has negotiated a 30 percent kill fee, you should pardon the expression."

Merilee pulled the plug on the bathtub and started to climb out. "I'm going to rinse off in the shower before I turn into a boiled lobster. Care to join me?"

"You talked me into it."

"You'll want to take off your T-shirt and boxer shorts first, not to mention your socks."

"I would have thought of that on my own, but thanks for mentioning it."

"Just part of my new plan, darling."

"Plan? What plan?"

"I'm obviously going to have to make more of an effort to hold on to you now that I have competition from my not-so-bashful cousin." She turned on the shower, adjusted the temperature, and climbed in.

I joined her, transfixed by the way the bubble bath suds streamed down her naked, perfectly toned body.

"Trust me, you don't have a thing to worry about."

"Would you like me to wash your back, darling?"

"I wouldn't say no."

She turned me around, reached for the soap, and began working a rich lather into the muscles of my back using a deep, circular motion.

I let out a sigh of contentment before I said, "Don't forget my front."

She turned me around and lathered up my chest and stomach, pausing for an agonizing moment before she got started farther south, working with infinite care and patience.

"I know I don't," she said.

"Don't what . . . ?"

"Have a thing to worry about."

"What makes you so sure?"

"Because you'd never, ever do anything to hurt Lulu."

"You make a very good point."

We did very little talking after that. Just rinsed off, dried off, and raced each other to bed, where I discovered I wasn't nearly as exhausted as I'd thought.

CHAPTER FIFTEEN

Lulu gave me a gentle nudge at 5:15 A.M. to let me know she needed to go out. She'd gotten very adept at rousing me to take her out for her predawn walk without waking up Merilee. She was very considerate that way. I wasted no time throwing on a Ramones T-shirt, jeans, a turtleneck sweater, and socks and tiptoed downstairs, rubbing the sleep from my eyes. Flicked on the vestibule light and put on my Chuck Taylor All Stars and shearling coat while Lulu waited not so patiently at the front door for me to hook her to her leash. Then I unlocked the door, and out we went into the January predawn darkness. It was windy and freezing outside. I should have put on a hat and gloves, but my hope was she'd take care of her business quickly, which is to say before frostbite set in.

Charlton Street was silent, excluding the gale-force wind. Lulu tugged me to the nearest tree—her tree—and emptied her bladder. Then she settled into a more leisurely pace as she worked her way from one neighboring house to the next before she found just the right spot to leave her morning deposit. I stood there yawning and shivering, my eyes still not fully open yet. In fact, I was so sleepy I hadn't noticed a car was idling across the street with its lights off. Who idles on Charlton Street at what was now five thirty on a frigid morning with their lights off? My immediate reaction was that it meant trouble. I fumbled for my house keys, fingers numb from the cold, and began tugging Lulu back home as fast as I could when the car's driver blinked his lights on and off and I realized it was an unmarked Crown Vic police cruiser.

Lieutenant Golden rolled down his window and called out, "Join me. It's nice and warm in here. I've got hot coffee and fresh hot bagels from a twenty-four-hour bakery on the Lower East Side."

I needed no more coaxing. Crossed the street, opened the passenger door, and got in, rubbing my hands together as Lulu climbed in between us. Golden handed me a blessedly hot takeout coffee cup. I took a grateful gulp, warming my hands on the cup.

"Couldn't remember if you took it black or regular," he said.

"Black's fine."

"Good. And not to worry, I brought six cups, although I've already gone through two of them waiting for you to walk Lulu."

"Up kind of early, aren't you?"

"I've been up all night. Couldn't sleep."

"Is this case getting to you?"

"Hoagy, I'm getting nowhere. I've got too many suspects and too many motives going off in too many directions. It's starting to whirl round and round in my head like a merry-go-round gone amok. Every time I try to slow it down, it speeds back up. It's driving me out of my mind."

"Sounds as if the inside of your head is like the climax of *Strangers on a Train*."

"Okay, I don't know what you're talking about."

"It's an old Hitchcock film. Never mind."

"I'm so stressed out that when Abby and I were doing the dinner dishes last night, I had my first migraine headache since I was in high school. Everything started getting all blurry and swirly, with those damned flashbulbs going off in front of my eyes. I took three Tylenols and stretched out with a cold cloth over my eyes. My vision went back to normal after a couple of hours, but my head wouldn't stop spinning and I couldn't get to sleep. I didn't want to wake up Abby, so I threw on some clothes and took off. Didn't even shave," he grumbled, thumbing his stubbly chin. "Oh, hey, have a bagel." He produced a paper bag of fragrant onion bagels from the floor at his feet. "Have as many as you want. If you buy a dozen, they give you one free."

I fished my Swiss Army knife from my jeans, reached into the bag, and grabbed one, glancing around.

"What are you looking for?"

"The cream cheese."

"You are such a goy from Connecticut. You don't slice open fresh, hot bagels and put cream cheese on them. You just chomp on them."

"Thank you for imparting your ethnic wisdom." I took a bite. He was right, of course. It was chewy and delicious. "Not that I don't appreciate this early morning catering service, but how did you end up here?"

"Simple. You're the smartest guy I know."

"I am? There's a frightening thought."

"I need to run it with you." He glanced at me uneasily. "You don't mind, do you?"

"No, not at all. First, let's catch up. The last time we spoke was on the sidewalk outside of Mona's apartment. I wanted to do some research for my article on Junior for SHE, and you were heading off to speak to Siena Bing and Jon Porterfield."

"Correct," he said, slurping his coffee. "Jeez, you should see her apartment. It looks like a Bloomingdale's showroom. Totally perfect. Totally impersonal. She was huddled on the sofa under a blanket, coughing, feverish, and not making a whole lot of sense. Kept talking about little white houses, picket fences, and daffodils. It's possible she stuck that knife in Mona's eye, but I'm not sure she's well enough—unless she was putting on an act for my benefit. I don't know. I just don't know."

"I know that she's not to be trusted. Don't forget, I tipped her off that Junior's autopsy had turned up that he was HIV positive and suggested she get tested. She told me she was afraid to. Yet you found out she'd known she was HIV positive for two weeks."

He nodded his head somewhat convulsively, making me wonder how many cups of coffee he'd really downed while he was waiting for me to get up. "She tried to explain that away yesterday by telling me she was afraid word would get out and her real estate agency would drop her."

"Did you believe her?"

He shrugged. "I did and I didn't."

"Mona told me that Junior was being hassled by another woman with whom he'd had a fling. Someone clingy. It was over as far as he was concerned. Siena told me her thing with Junior had just been a quickie, as in nothing special. It's possible she lied about that, too. Maybe she really loved the guy and killed him not only because he gave her the virus but because he dumped her for Mona. And then she evened the score by killing Mona, too. Does that play?"

Golden munched on another bagel, mulling it over. "She's thirty-six years old, is likely to get full-blown AIDS, and therefore has no picket fences and daffodils to look forward to. That would mean these were both revenge killings. It definitely plays."

"Remember I told you I'm positive I was followed from the phone book center at Grand Central to Mona's place in Hell's Kitchen? Was Siena feeling well enough to pull that off?"

"Maybe she didn't have to be. Maybe she followed Junior there days ago, already knew where Mona lived, and caught a cab there from her apartment. I did ask the doorman whether she's left her apartment in the past couple of days. He said she has the flu and hasn't gone anywhere. Gets food deliveries from Gristedes."

"Those guys aren't infallible," I said. "Maybe she slipped out and he didn't notice."

"It's also possible he saw her and didn't recognize her. I barely did. She was incredibly put together at Junior's murder scene. Not a hair out of place. Yesterday she looked like a bag lady."

I mulled it over. "I could buy that, but it doesn't explain away that someone followed me to Mona's apartment. Lulu definitely picked up a familiar scent when we came out of that bodega around the corner from her place with the six-pack of Pabst."

"Damn, you're right," he said disgustedly.

"How did your conversation go with Jon?"

"You first. What was your take on him?"

"Well, he's definitely near the top of my list of guys who I'd never want to see naked, right up there with Stormin' Gorman Thomas of the Milwaukee Brewers."

"Can we skip past that part?"

"Gladly. I think he downplayed how furious he was at Junior for wrecking his relationship with this woman in London named Cynthia. He was very serious about her. Practically engaged. Yet when he walked in on the two of them going at it in his bed at a dinner party, he immediately placed all of the blame on Cynthia, not Junior, and broke up with her. He told me you have to make special allowances for the Junior Singletons of the world, which just didn't ring true to me. There's a limit to how far hero worship goes. Jon had a solid motive for sticking that knife in Junior's eye."

Golden said, "Right. Jon's also the one who gave you the lead on Mona. He could have followed you from his office to SHE magazine, where you went after you talked to him, correct?"

"Correct."

"And then from Grand Central to Mona's apartment. What if it was Jon who was following you? What if he stuck Mona in the eye?"

"Why would he do that? Junior was already dead."

"Same reason as Siena. A revenge killing. I've seen it happen."

"Was Jon defensive or edgy when you spoke to him yesterday?"

"Not at all. He was calm and composed." Golden reached for another bagel. "Okay, now the merry-go-round in my head stops at Katie Healey, whose teenaged daughter, Bridget, Junior defiled and knocked up. She had motive. She had opportunity . . ."

"But she had zero motive for killing Mona. I doubt she even knew who Mona was, unless I'm totally missing something, which I admit is possible."

"No, I'm with you," Golden said. "I don't see any connection there. Plus, Bridget seems happy as a clam about what went down. She's not only getting married, but she cleared twenty-five thou. Life is good." He chewed on his bagel. "Next, the merry-go-round stops at our climate scientist, Jill Perlo, who had every reason for hating Junior's guts. He cut off her funding when she refused to sleep with him, what with her being in a committed relationship with another woman. He even changed her computer codes and tried to lock her out of her own research. Would you call that reason enough to kill the guy?"

"I would," I said. "Except how did she gain access to the steak knives? Was she ever in the town house? And why would she kill Mona?"

Golden didn't answer me. Just sat there in bewildered silence. I sincerely hoped he wasn't getting another migraine. After a long moment, he said, "Next, there's Barry Zallinger, the eye doctor, who harbored definite ill will toward Junior for being an unrepentant cheat and breaking Phoebe's heart."

"But why would he go after Mona? Besides, Barry has been two-timing Phoebe himself with his optician, Elvia, whom he yearns for and is no doubt still boinking now that Phoebe has dumped his sleazy ass."

"That word keeps sticking in my mind," Golden confessed.

"What word, ass?"

"No, sleazy. There's an acute shortage of genuinely sleazy people in this case, which keeps throwing me off balance. I'm used to dealing with the lowest of the low. Killers for hire. Gangbangers. Mobsters. Everyone in this case seems like a solid citizen."

"What about Chantelle's pimp Breeze and her dealer Ray-Ray?"

"See, I don't figure they're involved. The East Sixties isn't their scene. If one of them bumped off Junior, there'd be signs of forced entry, prints. Plus, there's no apparent link to Mona."

"You make a good point, Lieutenant. But I can throw someone faintly sleazy at you, if you'd like."

"Please do."

"Tiffany Tatum, Pippa Longworth's assistant, who stole a Yale classmate's term paper draft, lied about it, and got drop-kicked out of school. Even though she happens to be a great-looking babe who smells like Audrey Hepburn, she's sleazy. And, get this, when I was at the SHE office, I asked her if she knew Junior."

"And . . . ?"

"She blushed. As in got super uncomfortable."

"You think she was boinking him?"

"Something was going on between them. By the way, Pippa has a case of the hots for you. Wanted to know if you were available. She complained that age-appropriate men don't want to date her."

"Wait, how old is she?"

"Let's do the math. Her daughter Phoebe is twenty-seven. It's possible she's under fifty but more likely that she's fifty-two or so."

"You kidding me? She doesn't even look forty. How is that possible?"

"Are you familiar with Dr. Feelgood, that dodgy character who shoots up the Truman Capote Fifth Avenue crowd with happy-happy drugs?"

"I've heard about him. So?"

"So Merilee told me there's a new dodgy character in town who's called Dr. Lookgood. He injects non–FDA-approved serums such as Botox and collagen into the faces of rich socialites like Pippa. The injections remove age lines and furrows and give them plump young lips again."

"That's truly sick," he said before he fell into brooding silence. It was starting to get light out now, and the occasional car passed by.

"Is the merry-go-round still spinning around and around?" I asked.

"Hell, yeah. It never stops. Who else have you got?"

"Another candidate who's been staring us in the face all along—Phoebe herself. She's not necessarily the gentle fawn we've taken her for. She got strange on me last night."

"Strange as in . . . ?"

"Told me she had a mad crush on me. This was after she rubbed her pelvis against mine and stuck her tongue in my mouth."

"You're kidding me."

"I wish I were. She apologized profusely later. Said she was just incredibly scared and alone and her life was a total mess. All of which is true."

"Where did this happen?"

"I took her up to my apartment on West Ninety-Third. She got booted from the place where she's been staying, so I offered to let her stay in mine while she's figuring things out. She feels as if she's crowding us here. Merilee and I did just get married, although it's starting to feel as if I imagined that whole thing. We haven't been alone since we said 'I do.'"

"Where was Merilee while Phoebe was coming on to you?"

"At Elaine's with Robert Altman, the director, who she said is an alcoholic egomaniac and total prick."

"I'm sorry to hear that. I really liked *M*A*S*H.*" Golden thumbed his chin, brooding. "I've avoided saying much to you about Phoebe because she's Merilee's cousin and her whole life has been blown to pieces. But I've considered her a prime suspect all along, aside from the fact that I haven't an iota of proof linking her to either murder. Damn!" He slammed the dashboard with the palm of his hand, startling Lulu. "Why can't I make any sense of this crazy case?"

I finished off my third bagel before I said, "I picked up something yesterday that may make it even crazier."

"You have another suspect?"

"Possibly, but I can't be sure. I was going to call you about it this morning because I can't access the information I need on my own. That'll take someone with a badge, such as you."

"Give it up," he demanded impatiently. "Who's the suspect?"

"Bettie Page."

"Wait, who?"

"Bettie Page, the iconic fifties nude model. Remember all those Sherry-Netherland Hotel phone messages that were stuffed in the pocket of Junior's duffel coat?"

"Oh, right, right. But you said there was no way he could have been involved with her because she's got to be at least sixty years old. Plus, she became an Evangelical Christian disciple of Billy Graham's."

"Correct, right before she was diagnosed as a paranoid schizophrenic and was placed in a state psychiatric hospital."

"So what on earth does she have to do with this?"

"My guess is that 'Bettie Page' was his clingy girlfriend's semi-cute alias because she didn't want to leave her actual name with the hotel operator. And since she called him repeatedly, that suggests he wasn't calling her back, which had to be making her even clingier. Not to mention pissing her off."

"Okay, but where are you going with this?"

"I collected a possible piece of evidence yesterday that may point to who our needy, clingy girlfriend is. But you'll have to be the one to show it to the concierge at the Sherry-Netherland. It's a discreet, high-end hotel. I'll get nowhere with him. I have the evidence inside in my office. Why don't you come in the house and I'll fetch it for you. Besides, I need to feed Lulu her breakfast . . ." She let out an eager whoop. "Plus, you've been sitting out here for God knows how many hours, downing one coffee after another. You must need to pee desperately."

"Nah, I'm good. I always keep an empty gallon water jug in my trunk."

"Okay, I really didn't need to know that."

"But I wouldn't mind washing my hands."

"And I wouldn't dream of stopping you. Let's head inside."

He hesitated, making no move to open his door.

I studied him curiously. "Lieutenant, why are you really here?"

"Because I'm going to get yanked off of this case if I don't have a suspect in custody by the end of the day."

"And . . . ?"

"What makes you think there's an 'and'?"

"There's always an 'and.'"

"And whoever's behind this is crafty and smart, which means I need the help of someone who's even craftier and smarter. I'm desperate, okay? Lieutenant Mitry told me you broke his Oakmont case for him not only because of your smarts but because you employed an unconventional method that he was totally opposed to at first, but that it worked."

"That's correct, it did—with a couple of disclaimers. One, it was Lulu who cracked it, not me. Two, a state trooper took a bullet in the arm. And that's not even counting the part about me being rushed to the hospital for emergency surgery, but that's a whole other plot."

"This is serious. Stop kidding around."

"Trust me, I'm not."

"Okay, you're not. He told me you positioned the pieces in place so that the killer was revealed. This isn't easy for me to admit, but I'd like to talk over with you how you did it."

"Fine, okay. But first you need to take that new evidence to the Sherry-Netherland, because I believe it's the missing piece, and there's no point in discussing anything until you find out whether I'm right. While you're doing that, I have to get in my aquatic therapy. We can meet up at, say, ten o'clock in the lobby of the Racquet and Tennis Club. I'd also suggest you shave and put on fresh clothes. If I'm right, you're going to get a lot of media attention today. You'll be the detective who caught the Society Slayer. Have you got a navy blue suit?"

"I've got a real sharp double knit that's almost navy blue. It's what they call dark mauve."

"Which means . . . ?"

"It has a touch of purple in it."

"Just exactly how big of a touch?"

"I've got a patterned tie that matches it perfectly and a hot-pink shirt. Why are you looking at me that way?"

"When this case is closed, you and I need to have a serious talk about your wardrobe. But we've got a lot of work to do first. Come on, let's go inside. Lulu's hungry, and you may not need to pee, but I do."

Merilee was still asleep, the house dark except for the vestibule light. I turned on the kitchen light and put down Lulu's breakfast of succulent 9Lives mackerel, used the powder room, and left the light on for Golden so he could wash his hands. Then I tiptoed up the stairs quietly to my third-floor office. Our bedroom door was closed, with no sign of a light on under the door. It wasn't 7:00 A.M. yet, and Merilee was still asleep. So was Phoebe, it appeared.

I fetched the evidence from my desk, tucked it in a manila envelope, and brought it down to Golden, who was waiting in the vestibule. "There's a magazine article in here and a photograph I've cut out. Ask the concierge if he recognizes the person in that photograph as someone who visited Junior there."

Golden stared at the envelope but didn't open it. "Okay . . ."

"Also find out from whoever took the Bettie Page phone messages how old the woman who kept calling Junior sounded—young, middle-aged, older . . ."

"That matters?"

"It matters. I'll see you at the Racquet and Tennis Club at ten. If you're running late, I'll be waiting for you in the lobby."

He reached for the doorknob and stopped. "Hoagy, if this blows up in my face, I'll end up on traffic detail in Bensonhurst."

"That's just occurring to you now?"

"No, it's been on my mind all night."

"Do you want to back out?"

"No . . ."

"You sure?"

"Positive."

"Good answer. Breathe deep, Lieutenant. You're about to become a hero."

CHAPTER SIXTEEN

I made two steaming cups of espresso, carried them upstairs to our room, and flicked on my nightstand lamp.

Merilee stirred, plumped her pillows, and sat up with a sleepy grin. "You know what? You're the best husband I've ever had. Also the only husband I've ever had, unless you count the seven days I was married to Dennis Hopper."

"I happen to know you're fibbing. You were married to Ernie Borgnine. And it was eight days, not seven."

"I can't put anything over on you, can I?"

"Don't even try, Blondie."

She sipped her espresso. "I was half-asleep, but I swear I heard voices when you were rustling around downstairs. Is Lulu learning how to speak?"

"No, that was a rumpled, unshaven Lieutenant Golden. He was idling outside in his cruiser with coffee and a bag of fresh, hot onion bagels when I took Lulu out for her predawn walk. The poor guy was up all night. This case is driving him crazy."

"What did he want from you?"

"My advice. He's not used to society slayings. He's more accustomed to a higher class of people, such as gangbangers. So we sat in his cruiser with the heater on, drank coffee, ate bagels, and talked. Did you know that if a bagel is fresh and hot, you don't put cream cheese on it? You just eat it."

"I did not."

"That makes us both a couple of real goys."

Lulu climbed up onto the bed and curled up next to Merilee, her tail thumping.

Merilee sipped some more espresso, stroking her. "Were you able to give him any advice?"

"Possibly. I gave him a piece of evidence I collected yesterday that may prove to be helpful. In fact, I'm positive it will. He's going to run it down, then stop off at home to shave and put on fresh clothes while I do my laps in the pool at the Club. Have you ever heard of a color called dark mauve?"

"I can't say that I have. Why?"

"That's the color of the clean, unrumpled double knit suit he'll be wearing. He has one of his lobster-bib ties and a hot-pink shirt that go with it."

"I can't believe the woman in his life lets him leave the house dressed that way."

"Her name is Abby. She's a former pole dancer."

Merilee's face it up. "Really? I've always wanted to learn how to pole dance. It's supposed to be great exercise."

"Kind of a major turn-on, too."

She batted her eyes at me. "I wouldn't know a thing about that."

"Well, I would. Then he's going to meet me at the Club, and we'll strategize."

"When you say strategize, you don't mean you're concocting another scheme like you did in Oakmont, are you?"

"The subject did come up. It seems that Lieutenant Mitry still can't say enough nice things about me."

"Did you tell Lieutenant Golden that you came within a quarter inch of getting killed?"

"Don't exaggerate. It was a half inch. What I told him was that I didn't crack the case, Lulu did."

Lulu let out a low whoop. I rubbed her belly.

"Hoagy, I'm not liking the sound of this."

"Not to worry. Nothing has been settled yet."

"Do you have a scheme?"

"Sure."

"Then I have every reason to worry. I suppose you're going to tell me to keep this evening free."

"Actually, it'll be more like this afternoon."

"And that the same will hold true for Phoebe."

"As a matter of fact, it will."

"Does this mean you know who the killer is?"

"At this point, it only qualifies as an educated guess."

"Does not. You do know, otherwise you wouldn't be 'strategizing' with Lieutenant Golden."

I let that slide by. "What are your plans for this morning?"

"A few minutes before you arrived with my coffee, Phoebe tiptoed down here, woke me up, and asked me to help her move into your apartment. Shouldn't take long. All she needs is her violin, her music stand, and a suitcase of clothes."

"She's really serious about this?"

"She really is. She's incredibly excited. Why, are you having second thoughts about letting her use it?"

"No, not at all." I fished my keys from the pocket of my jeans and put them on her nightstand. "I'm mostly concerned that she's accustomed to living in a nicer neighborhood in a place that has heat."

"She loves the place. Thinks it's like a Parisian garret. Besides, all she wants is to be left alone to play her violin where nobody knows her and Pippa won't bother her."

"Makes perfect sense when you put it that way," I said before I got busy.

I stowed my barley tweed suit from Strickland & Sons, a pale yellow shirt, Grandfather's martini glass cuff links, and a muted burgundy tie in my folding garment bag. My swim trunks and goggles went in my briefcase in their waterproof plastic bag. Then I went in the bathroom and shaved. Put my Ramones T-shirt, turtleneck sweater, and jeans back on but switched from my Chuck Taylor All Stars to my kid leather ankle boots. Then I gathered up my things and kissed Merilee goodbye. A long, lingering kiss.

Her eyes searched mine. "Darling, are we ever going to make it to the Enchanted Cottage?"

"Very soon."

"Tomorrow?"

"Tonight."

"Are you pulling my leg?"

"I'd love nothing better, but I'm on a rather tight schedule."

"Shall I tell Rocco to reserve that Land Rover for us?"

"Go right ahead."

"When this nightmare is over, I'll really need the Enchanted Cottage."

"We both will." I heard a soft yip. "Which is to say all three of us."

Merilee's eyes sparkled at me. "I've never been on a honeymoon before."

"Ernie didn't take you on one? What a cheapskate."

◆

I had the pool to myself again that morning. My self-appointed lifeguard trotted alongside me, barking her head off as I swam lap after lap, and I felt the Australian crawl stretch out and strengthen my shoulder. Soon, the injury would be only a memory, aside from the surgical scars. I ruminated as I swam, working my way through all the people who were riding those horses on Lieutenant Golden's high-speed merry-go-round. So many of them had motives for wanting Junior dead. Too many. That's what was driving Golden crazy. But which one had wanted Mona dead, too? Mona's murder was the tell as to who'd stabbed Junior in the eyeball with the first of those two rosewood-handle steak knives that Katie Healey kept razor sharp every two weeks.

When I'd done my forty-five minutes, I climbed out of the pool, panting, removed my goggles, patted Lulu, and gasped, "Good work, girl." Rinsed off, toweled off, and unzipped my garment bag. Dressed in my shirt and tie, suit, and ankle boots. Ran a comb through my hair. Stowed my swimming trunks and goggles back in their sealed plastic bag, which went in my garment bag along with my jeans and turtleneck. Then I headed for the lobby. It was a few minutes past ten.

Lieutenant Golden was waiting there for me, pacing impatiently with the envelope I'd given him tucked under his arm and a grim expression on his face. He'd shaved and donned his dark mauve—which is to say purple—double knit suit, matching lobster-bib tie, and hot-pink shirt. I had an overwhelming desire to make a bonfire out of his entire wardrobe, but something told me it was nonflammable and would merely melt into a sticky puddle of Oobleck. And if you don't recall what Oobleck is, then you should be spending more of your evenings rereading Dr. Seuss and less time watching *Dallas*.

I fetched my shearling coat and fedora from the coatroom. His cruiser was parked outside. I tossed my garment bag on the back seat and we got in, Lulu in her customary spot between us. The lieutenant still hadn't said a single word.

"So . . . ?" I finally asked him.

"The concierge at the Sherry-Netherland identified the photo right away," he responded, narrowing his gaze at me. "How did you know?"

"Because it was the only way it made any sense."

"I agree, but what's your plan? We're not dealing with idiots here. No one will say a single word without a lawyer present."

"You told me that Lieutenant Mitry advised you to put yourself in my hands, or words to that effect."

Golden stuck out his lower lip. "True . . ."

"Did he tell you what that entails?"

"He did. And I don't like it."

"He didn't either," I said. "Is this a go or not? Because if you'd prefer to pursue it by conventional means, just say so. I won't be offended. In fact, I'll be thrilled. Merilee and I will be able to leave right away for our long-overdue honeymoon in Vermont."

He sat there in tight silence for a long moment. "I'm afraid that's not going to happen. I've already set the wheels in motion. I have a dozen men rounding up each and every suspect. They'll be ready and waiting at Phoebe's town house at noon. Two men are on the way out to Rockaway Beach to pick up Katie and Bridget Healey. If they hit traffic, they may be a few minutes late, but everyone else will be there."

"Has anyone offered any resistance so far?"

"Dr. Barry Zallinger."

"Why am I not surprised?"

"It seems that he has a noon appointment with a patient. But he's going to try to rearrange his schedule."

"That's mighty big of him. Anyone else?"

"No one."

"Of course not. They wouldn't dare."

He exhaled and said, "Hoagy, are you sure this is going to work?"

"Why, are you getting cold feet?"

"We aren't dealing with idiots here," he said once again.

"It doesn't matter how smart they are. Or wealthy. Or sophisticated. They'll all shrivel up into tiny balls of terror when their personal secrets are revealed aloud in front of the others, not to mention your men in uniform standing there glowering at them. Just remember: The password is fear."

"Fear," he repeated.

"I suggest you arrive a few minutes late just to make everyone sweat. Merilee, Lulu, and I will be ten minutes late."

"What's the strategy behind that?"

"There isn't any. Merilee is always ten minutes late."

"You were serious about having one of my men bring Phoebe, right? She won't be coming with you?"

"Correct. That wouldn't send a good message to the others."

"Understood."

"Since it'll be lunchtime, do you think we should provide sandwiches and coffee?"

"Pippa Longworth is seeing to that. Her assistant, Tiffany, will order a dozen assorted sandwiches from a deli on Madison near their office."

"I hope she gets a liverwurst. I'm in the mood for liverwurst."

"Thanks for sharing that. And someone at the house will make coffee."

"Excellent. I have a very good feeling about this."

Lulu let out a yip.

"More importantly, so does my lifeguard."

"Your what?"

"My lifeguard. When I swim laps, she runs alongside the pool and—"

"You know what? Forget I asked. I don't want to know the answer."

"Is it just me or are you getting grumpy, Lieutenant?"

"Do me a favor, will you? Grab your garment bag and your puppy and get the hell out of my car."

"Definitely grumpy."

CHAPTER SEVENTEEN

There were four police cruisers double-parked in front of the town house where we'd found Junior Singleton's body on his dressing room floor with a Claude Dozorme rosewood steak knife plunged into his left eyeball—the discovery that had set off a nightmarish journey into the murder of Mona Dale with a second knife from the same set, along with side excursions into the AIDS virus, heroin abuse, Strutters' Walk, teen pregnancy, Phoebe's breakup with Dr. Barry Zallinger, and the end of her long association with the Brearley School.

Our cab delivered Merilee, Lulu, and me ten minutes late, as I'd expected. It was exceptionally fragrant in the house. Phoebe was in the kitchen brewing coffee in a twelve-cup electric coffee maker while Tiffany was arranging a platter of deli sandwiches on the dining table—tragically, none were liverwurst. Siena was setting out plates and coffee cups. The air was also scented with Tiffany's Audrey Hepburn perfume.

Siena had worked hard to look her best. She'd dressed in a Ralph Lauren navy blue pantsuit. She'd washed and brushed out her hair and applied makeup to the circles under her eyes as well as a bit of toner to her cheeks to bring back that sun-kissed glow. But she was ill, and there was no getting around it. The light had gone out of her eyes, and she was moving in slo-mo, as if she'd been possessed by Count Dracula.

Phoebe, who'd spent the morning moving into my apartment, was wearing her shawl-collar cardigan and jeans. Merilee, who'd helped her with the move, was wearing an old black cashmere turtleneck of mine, jeans, and cowboy boots. She got busy setting out napkins and water glasses on the glass-topped steamer-trunk coffee table in the living room. Her aunt Pippa, who today wore a champagne-colored

Gucci ruffle neck silk top and matching gabardine slacks, did not feel the least bit obliged to pitch in. Just sat there on one of the leather sofas with her arms crossed, staring into the fire that was crackling in the fireplace, and looking extremely put out about having to be there.

Two patrolmen stood by the French doors to the garden with their own arms crossed, silent and serious. I'd noticed two more seated in one of the cruisers outside.

Tiffany, who seemed extremely nervous, was wearing pleated gray flannel slacks and a royal blue crew neck sweater. Lulu kept following her around the kitchen, yipping and yapping at her, craving her attention.

"Why is she doing that?" Tiffany asked me.

"She likes you," I said, smiling at her.

Tiffany bent down and gave Lulu's ears a gentle tug. "And I like you, too, sweetie. In fact, your mommy and daddy had better watch out or I'm going to smuggle you out in my shoulder bag."

Several others had arrived, though there was a total absence of chatter among them. The rotund British investment broker, Jon Porterfield, who was sharing a sofa with Pippa, had raided the sandwich platter and was devouring a thick corned beef sandwich with Swiss cheese and Russian dressing, being careful not to drip any of that Russian dressing on the charcoal Savile Row double-breasted suit that artfully contained his girth. Dr. Barry Zallinger, the Fifth Avenue ophthalmologist who'd broken Phoebe's heart, wasn't eating or sitting, just standing like a glum wallflower next to the fireplace with his hands buried in the pockets of his permanent-press slacks. Since this was the lunch hour, it was possible that his body clock was thrown off, that he was yearning for the naked flesh of Elvia, and that a sandwich was the last thing on his mind.

Possibly, he couldn't imagine why he'd been summoned there. Then again, possibly he could.

The most brilliant person in the room, climate scientist Jill Perlo, was seated at the far end of the sofa that faced Pippa and Jon's across the coffee table, scribbling notes in a lab book while she calmly waited for this event, whatever it was, to be over and done with. She wore a ski sweater, coarse wool pants, and hiking boots.

Merilee sat down not far from Jill, and Lulu immediately joined her, tail thumping.

Katie and Bridget Healey were the last to arrive.

"Sorry, sir," a patrolman said to Lieutenant Golden, who'd been waiting for them outside in his cruiser. "There was traffic on the LIE like you wouldn't believe."

"No problem. Join us, ladies."

"Why, it's Katie and Bridget." Phoebe smiled at the housekeeper and her daughter as they entered the kitchen. "Hello! We've got sandwiches and coffee, and everyone is gathering in the living room."

"Need help, hon?" Katie asked her.

"No, thanks. I'm fine. Besides, you're not here to work."

"Why am I here?"

"Your guess is as good as mine."

Bridget, who was eating for two, grabbed a turkey sandwich on her way into the living room, gasping when she saw Merilee seated there. "Omigod, I love you! Can I have your autograph?"

"Certainly," Merilee said graciously. "But why don't we wait until later? It seems we have some business to take care of first."

"Sure thing. I mean, okay."

Everyone found a place to sit on one of the two sofas. I sat on a kitchen chair facing the sofas. Lieutenant Golden stood facing me over by the French doors to the patio, flanked by the two patrolmen in uniform. Two more patrolmen stood in the kitchen behind me.

Everyone who'd been delivered to the town house was behaving quietly and cooperatively—with the exception, not surprisingly, of Pippa.

"I demand to know what I'm doing here, Lieutenant!" she said angrily. "I happen to be a personal friend of Mayor Koch and am not accustomed to being hauled out of my office by a pair of jackbooted thugs. I have the right to have my lawyer present. Until he is, I refuse to sit here watching people stuff their faces on sandwiches while you conduct some sort of parlor game."

"It's not a game, Mrs. Longworth," Golden responded with tremendous gravity in his voice. "It's anything but that. So why don't you just climb down off your high horse and let the process unfold? If you decide you still want your lawyer present, you have that right."

She considered this in icy silence before she said, "I find this whole situation highly irregular."

"I don't disagree, but I felt that convening everyone here would be preferable to a caravan of patrol cars pulling up in front of the Nineteenth Precinct house filled with notable figures such as yourself and your niece, Miss Nash. Imagine your photographs on the front page of tomorrow morning's *New York Post,* which has photographers staked out across the street from the precinct house morning, noon, and night. This way is much more discreet."

"Okay, fine," she said brusquely. "But let's get on with it."

He glanced at me. "Want to take over?"

"Wait, why is he taking over?" Pippa demanded shrilly.

Golden took a slow breath in and out, maintaining his composure. "Because he's been caught in the middle of this, through no fault of his own, and because he knows all of you personally. He's even related to you and your daughter by marriage."

"That's right." Merilee beamed at me. "We're married."

"Also because Hoagy has a gifted novelist's insights into the dark depths of human behavior," Golden added. "That's not exactly the strong suit of the police mind, which tends to be governed by rules and procedures. His mind doesn't work that way. Frankly, I don't exactly understand how it works. But he finds patterns that the rest of us don't. It may surprise you to learn he has been helpful in the recent past as a consultant to the Connecticut State Police."

"Along with my short-legged partner," I pointed out.

Lulu thumped her tail as she lay stretched out between Merilee and Phoebe. Joining them on the sofa were Katie, Bridget, and Jill. Pippa sat directly across the coffee table from Phoebe on the other sofa, flanked by Jon, Tiffany, Siena, and Barry, who'd finally consented to sit down.

"I'm missing *Jezebel* on Channel Eleven with Bette Davis," Katie said to me unhappily. "It's one of my favorites."

"I apologize. I appreciate you coming, as does the lieutenant."

"I certainly didn't have much of a choice," Jon said crossly. "A patrolman showed up in my office and ordered me here. I had to ask my assistant to reschedule my entire afternoon before I was whisked out the door."

"In response to Pippa's query," I said, "the reason we're here is to have a conversation about what's transpired since Merilee and I got married at city hall Tuesday morning and Phoebe, who served as one our witnesses, persuaded us to have a look at this wonderful town house, which became hers after she and Junior finalized their divorce and she decided to sell it. Siena, who's the property's Realtor, can attest that it's one of the premier luxury properties in Manhattan's most desirable neighborhood, and would no doubt have been sold within two or three days. We were planning to go away that afternoon to spend a week in Vermont on our honeymoon. Phoebe, who wanted us to buy it, pleaded with us to hop in a cab and come take a look. So we did, figuring we'd still have enough time to make it to Brattleboro before dark."

"Brattleboro?" Pippa said incredulously. "That's where you were planning to spend your honeymoon?"

"Still is," Merilee said brightly.

"Not exactly chic, is it?"

"Unlike you, Aunt Pippa, I don't live my life by what's chic or not chic. My aunt Betsy, who's my father's oldest sister, has the dearest, sweetest cottage outside of town in the apple orchards. I loved it when I was a little girl. I called it the Enchanted Cottage. I still do. And I've always fantasized that if I was ever lucky enough to marry the man of my dreams that we would spend our honeymoon there."

"That's so sweet," young Bridget spoke up. "I mean, God, you're rich enough to go somewhere like Tahiti. I'm really happy for you that your dream came true."

Merilee smiled at her. "I'm glad you understand. I'm afraid my aunt Pippa doesn't, and never will."

Pippa glared across the coffee table at her. "Why would you say something like that?"

"Because you have a heart of stone, Pippa. Always have, always will."

"I don't mean to be rude," Barry spoke up, "but I've already had to cancel one patient today, and I really don't want to cancel another. Can we please get on with why we're here?"

"Absolutely," I said. "As the days have gone by, it has turned out that each of you either had a reason to want Junior dead or had a close personal relationship with someone who did. What's been puzzling me is who would want his lover, Mona Dale, the former lead singer of Four Hundred Blows, dead. Hardly anyone knew that he and Mona were lovers, or that he spent nearly every night with her in her basement apartment in Hell's Kitchen instead of his luxury suite at the Sherry-Netherland."

I had everyone's attention now. Those who'd been eating stopped chewing. Just stared at me, waiting to hear what I was going to say next.

"It was quite a shock," I recalled, "when we opened Junior's dressing room door and found him there dead on the floor with that steak knife plunged into his eyeball. It was also quite a shock that the police investigation indicated no sign of forced entry, meaning that whoever killed him either had a key to the house or was a friend of his whom he'd invited over." My gaze landed on Katie the housekeeper.

"What are you looking at me for?" she demanded.

"Because you claimed you didn't come to work that day."

"Which I didn't," she insisted.

"And because two months ago, Junior had unprotected sex with your nineteen-year-old daughter, Bridget, when she was subbing for you and got her pregnant. He offered to pay for an abortion, but she's a good Catholic girl who doesn't believe in abortion—so Junior gave her $25,000 for her medical expenses instead. As Bridget told the lieutenant and me yesterday, she and her fiancé, Tommy the firefighter, are getting married on Saturday."

"Congratulations, Bridget," Merilee said warmly.

Bridget blushed. "Thanks."

"Tommy is aware that she's pregnant," I said. "But he has no idea that he's not the father of the child."

"Never will, either," Katie said with great conviction.

Bridget said, "And I'll never be sorry about what happened. I had such a crush on Junior. He was so dreamy."

"There she goes again," Katie muttered. "He wasn't dreamy. He was a rich bastard who thought he was entitled to take whoever he wanted. Well, guess what? This time, Junior paid for the way he treated women."

"Is that what you think happened to him?" I asked her.

"You bet it is," she replied. "I can't prove it. I just know it."

"We were absolutely flabbergasted the morning after his murder," I continued, "when the medical examiner reported that his autopsy revealed Junior was HIV positive. He had the AIDS virus. Not that this came as news to Siena, who'd had unprotected sex with him a few weeks earlier when he stopped by the house to clear out some of his possessions. It wasn't long before Siena started feeling poorly." I gazed at her. "You were clearly suffering from flu-like symptoms when we took our house tour on Tuesday and found Junior's body."

Siena's eyes avoided my gaze, her jaw tightening.

"I met Siena for coffee, tipped her off about the medical examiner's findings, and suggested she get tested right away, unaware that she already had two weeks earlier and was well aware that she was HIV positive. You lied to me, Siena, which I can understand. You didn't want your secret to get out in the small, competitive world in which you work. You'd be branded as undesirable and unable to get any listings. You, for one, had every reason to stick that steak knife in Junior's eye. He gave you a virus for which there is currently no cure."

Siena's eyes puddled with tears. "It's true. I'm going to die of AIDS."

"Don't talk that way," Jill Perlo scolded her. "Don't even think it. You've got access to the very best medical care in America. And the National Institutes of Health is finally springing into action in search of a treatment now that AIDS has entered the mainstream population—which is to say white heterosexuals," she added sourly. "Promise me you won't give up."

"I'll try," Siena said softly, her voice quavering.

I said, "What puzzles me, Siena, is how you found out about Mona and why you stabbed her in the eye with another knife from the same set. Can you shed any light on that?"

"I didn't stab her," she shot back angrily. "I didn't even know who she was. And I for damned sure didn't stab Junior. He meant nothing to me. We had one quick fuck, that's all. And I do mean quick. Just when I started to get heated up, he was already putting his pants back on."

Phoebe nodded glumly. "One of the great disappointments of my life was to discover that my husband cared only about his own pleasure. I thought of him as Mr. Bim-Bam-Boom. He was in. He was out. He was gone."

"I doubt he lasted two minutes with me," Bridget added, blushing. "He was done so fast it was practically an oopsie. Not like my Tommy. Tommy wants to share his love with me, so he takes his time. He's patient."

"We don't need to hear this kind of thing," Katie said to her angrily.

"Yes, we do," I said. "Do you have anything to add, Professor Perlo?"

She glared at me. "I told you that I'm in a committed same-sex relationship, remember?"

"Yet you had every reason for wanting him dead. When you refused to have sex with him on your rock climbing trip to Bryce Canyon, Utah, he retaliated by cutting off the funding for your Climate Science Center at Canterbury College that he'd so generously endowed. It was a nasty, petty thing to do, and certainly gave you a motive for getting even."

"He didn't give a damn about climate science," she responded bitterly. "He just wanted to get in my pants. But I didn't kill him. I've never even been in this house before. Besides, I'll find other sources of funding, even though the traditional scientific community is intolerant of my ideas and sexual orientation. That's fine by me. It just makes me want to fight them harder."

"Did Junior ever mention Mona to you?"

Jill shook her head. "Never."

I gazed into the fire for a moment before I turned to Tiffany and said, "You got rather uncomfortable when I mentioned Junior to you the day I visited the SHE offices. Were you another one of his conquests?"

"Why, no," she said, getting uncomfortable once again. "Never, I swear."

I peered at her. "I see." Next, I turned my attention to Phoebe. "After you and Junior split up, you became romantically involved with Dr. Zallinger, who was a member of your chamber music quartet."

Phoebe nodded. "He called me his 'Golden Goddess.' Could not believe that I was the least bit interested in him. But he was exactly the sort of man whom I needed after Junior. He was gentle, affectionate, and sensitive. We'd snuggle in bed together for hours. He'd stroke me and tell me how much he loved me."

"I do love you," Barry spoke up, his voice cracking.

"You're a two-timing liar," Phoebe said to him angrily. "Merilee told me the truth this morning while we were moving my things into Hoagy's apartment. You've been having an affair with Elvia, your married optician, for years, and kept right on having it while you were with me. That's why you didn't want me to move in with you. You're just as bad as Junior was. I hate you."

Barry cleared his throat, his significant Adam's apple bobbing up and down. "I told you about that in the strictest confidence," he said to me. "You swore you wouldn't tell anyone."

"I know I did, but Merilee's not 'anyone.' She's my wife. I refuse to keep secrets from her."

She reached over and squeezed my hand.

"Why am I here?" Barry demanded.

"Because you had a strong reason to harbor negative feelings toward Junior. He was cruel to the woman whom you claimed that you loved. He was also stabbed in the eyeball, and you happen to be an eye doctor. Maybe that's just a coincidence. Then again, maybe it's not."

"I had nothing to do with it," he insisted.

"Are you still seeing Elvia, or have you broken it off with her?"

"I don't see how that's relevant."

"Answer the question," Golden ordered him.

"She . . . quit, actually," he said. "Took a job with an optometrist in Teaneck. Her husband's optometrist, actually."

I stared at him. "When did this happen?"

"Yesterday."

"Rather sudden, wasn't it?"

"Very sudden."

"What prompted it?"

"I asked her to marry me."

"Not that you've ever sought me out for advice on love and marriage—no, come to think of it, you have—but that was a really dumb idea."

"Can we please just drop this subject?" he asked me rather mournfully.

"Not quite yet. How did Elvia respond to your proposal?"

"She turned me down, then told me she's been looking for a job closer to home for a while."

"Why is that?"

"Because she doesn't want to break up her marriage and family."

I said, "Wise woman."

"I'll have y-you know that I'm not the total cretin you seem to think I am," Barry sputtered angrily. "I'm a respected member of the medical community with a very successful practice."

"That won't be for long."

He glowered at me. "Why on earth would you say that?"

"Because now that you can no longer indulge in nooners with Elvia, for whom you yearn, you'll have to take on a new optician as soon as possible, preferably one who's young, attractive, and willing. You'll pursue her. She'll show no interest in sharing lunch, dinner, or a weekend in the Poconos with you, yet you'll keep after her until she decides to quit. The other women in your office will talk, same as they no doubt talked about you and Elvia. There are no secrets in a small office. But this time it won't be a consensual relationship. It'll be sexual harassment. Word will get out about it up and down the Fifth

Avenue medical offices within a week, which means you'll have trouble finding someone to replace her. Your practice will suffer. The office won't run as smoothly as it used to. You'll find yourself losing patients, also referrals. Tell me, where were you, say, eighteen to twenty-four hours before that steak knife was plunged into Junior's eyeball?"

"What day would that be?"

"Monday."

"I performed cataract surgery on two patients in the morning, had office hours in the afternoon, and that evening saw a classic French film, *The Wages of Fear,* with Phoebe at the Thalia."

I turned to Phoebe. "Does seeing the movie jibe with your memory?"

She nodded.

"So you're each other's alibis."

Her eyes widened. "Hoagy, you don't think I had anything to do with Junior's murder, do you?"

"No, of course not."

"Well, I didn't either," Barry said insistently. "I'm a doctor. A healer. I'm not a violent person."

"We're all violent if we get pissed off enough," I said, turning my attention next to Jon. "You and Junior were good friends. Used to hang out together when you were here in New York and when he was in England. You threw weekend parties at your country house in Devon that he enjoyed. You stiff-upper-lip Brits sure do know how to cut loose. Those parties of yours sounded more like orgies."

Jon ran a hand over his bald pink head. "And your point is . . . ?"

"You've described yourself to me as someone who's not exactly a lady-killer. You're affluent and well connected, but women don't seem to take a shine to you. Yet you developed a serious relationship with a young woman named Cynthia last year. You went away together for weekends. You met her parents. You were even considering marriage—until, that is, you threw a dinner party at your flat in London and found her naked in your bed with Junior."

Jon's face fell. "It's true, I did. But he wanted her, so he took her."

"Did they stay together long?"

"No. It was over and done with that night."

"You must have been furious."

He raised his chin at me. "I was. I thought Cynthia genuinely loved me, but she broke my heart. Said she'd had too much champers, that Junior was very persuasive, and that before she knew what hit her, they were between the sheets. She begged me to forgive her, but once the trust is gone, it's gone. I've never spoken to her again. Haven't returned her phone calls or answered her letters. I want nothing to do with her."

"Yet you remained friends with Junior. Weren't you angry at him?"

Jon shook his head. "Couldn't be. You have to make special allowances for the Junior Singletons of the world. Men who know no boundaries or restraints. He wanted Cynthia, so he took her. I didn't blame him. It was she who I was furious at."

"You, sir, are a sexist pig," Jill Perlo said to him.

"That's your opinion," he responded, unfazed.

"It's not an opinion, it's a statement of fact," she said. "He was allowed to do whatever he wanted, but she wasn't. Let me take a wild guess—you haven't been in a relationship with a woman since then."

Jon's mouth tightened. "I'll admit I have trouble trusting them."

"And they have trouble wanting to see you naked. God knows I wouldn't want to. Just the thought of it makes me shudder."

"Okay, okay, calm down," Golden said to her.

"I'm perfectly calm, Lieutenant," she assured him.

"You've been a fund of valuable information, Jon," I said. "It was you who told me about Junior's penchant for visiting Strutters' Walk, where Lieutenant Golden and I discovered that he'd been shooting heroin with a street hooker named Chantelle Williams, who is HIV positive and sick at home with her mom. We're pretty certain that he got exposed to the virus from her."

Jon let out a sigh of regret. "That's a real tragedy. But taking crazy risks was part of who he was."

"You also turned me on to his affair with Mona Dale, whom he met at the Department of Motor Vehicles."

Pippa frowned across the coffee table at me. "They were in line together?"

I shook my head. "She worked there. Became a civil servant after Four Hundred Blows broke up. They were a one-hit-wonder punk rock band. Mona, the lead singer, was a pink-haired vixen with a great body. Almost as big a sex symbol as Debbie Harry. Junior was a huge fan."

Jon nodded. "He was totally enthralled by her."

"After you and I spoke at your office, Jon, I went to the offices of SHE to discuss writing a cover story about Junior, whom Pippa told me she thought of as America's last great gentleman adventurer. After that, I went to Grand Central to look up Mona Dale in the phone books there. I found four Mona Dales in Manhattan, two living in wealthy neighborhoods, two not so much. I targeted those two and struck gold with my second call. She sounded very down, but told me she'd be willing to have me stop by her place in Hell's Kitchen. As I hung up and started toward Vanderbilt to catch a cab, I suddenly became seized by the certainty that I was being followed, even though Lulu, who's a world-class scent hound, wasn't on high alert at all. But we were surrounded by a sea of people on the floor of the terminal wearing a vast array of perfumes, colognes, and deodorants, not to mention standing near Zaro's Bakery and the Oyster Bar."

Merilee sighed. "I have a sudden craving for an Oyster Bar pan roast."

Lulu let out a whimper. Pan roasts were a particular favorite of hers, too.

"Mona had asked me to stop and pick up a six-pack of Pabst Blue Ribbon at a bodega on Eleventh Avenue near her place," I continued. "When I left the bodega, Pabst in hand, Lulu instantly raised her nose into the air and let out a yap. Now she smelled someone with whom we'd been in recent contact. Someone who'd tailed us there. I glanced around but didn't see anyone watching us. As we crossed Eleventh and walked along West Forty-Fifth Street, I kept looking behind us and scanning the sidewalk across the street, but whoever it was knew how to keep out of sight. When we visited the murder scene the next day with Lieutenant Golden, Lulu didn't pick up the scent there, which is critical. It means that whoever it was who followed us to Mona's apartment wasn't her killer. Just a private detective hired to tail me or, possibly, a slippery employee who was willing to do slippery chores for her employer. Am I right, Tiffany?"

Tiffany reddened. "Do I have to answer that?" she asked Pippa.

"No, you do not," Pippa answered with lofty certainty.

"That's okay," I said. "I'll just assume that you confirmed it was you. After all, Tiffany, it wasn't the first time you'd done something slippery for Pippa, which was why you got so uncomfortable when I mentioned Junior's name to you at the SHE office."

"Wait, what else did she do?" Golden asked.

"She provided the voice of 'Bettie Page' when 'Bettie' left all of those phone messages for Junior at the Sherry-Netherland. Messages that he never returned. After all, it was much more appropriate for a sweet young thing to be calling him up than a fifty-something bellower such as her employer, even if Pippa does pass for forty thanks to all of those treatments from Dr. Lookgood. Mona told me that he'd had a fling with a clingy, needy woman whom he couldn't get rid of. That clingy, needy woman was you, Pippa. You had an affair with your own daughter's husband."

"You slept with Junior?" Phoebe cried out at her mother in outrage.

Pippa maintained her composure, aside from swiping at some invisible crumbs in her lap. "Surely, you're not surprised. He slept with everyone."

"But you're my mother!"

"If you're angling for an apology, you're not going to get one. Junior and I were a lot alike. I take whatever and whomever I want, as did he. So why not? And we had ourselves some pretty terrific sex in his suite. I knew how to satisfy him. You didn't, or at least that's what he told me. He said you were a cold fish."

I turned to Merilee and said, "I'm overwhelmed by the mother-daughter love here, aren't you?"

Actually, Merilee was infuriated. "Pippa, you've been a cruel bitch for as long as I can remember," she said in an icy voice. "But sleeping with Junior was beyond indecent."

"How did you find out?" Pippa asked me. "Did Tiffany tell you?"

"Nope. I went to the magazine store in Times Square yesterday and rummaged through three years of back issues of SHE. Eighteen months ago, you ran a lengthy appreciation of Bettie Page and her trailblazing career. That explains how 'Bettie Page' popped up as your alias when you had Tiffany leave all those phone messages for Junior. It so happens that you run a flattering photo of yourself in every issue on your 'From the Editor' introductory page. I gave the photo to Lieutenant Golden this morning. He showed it to the concierge at the Sherry-Netherland and asked him if he recognized you. He did. He said you'd spent the night in Mr. Singleton's suite numerous times, though not lately. And the operator confirmed that it was a young voice that called and left the 'Bettie Page' phone messages. Your voice, Tiffany."

"Did I do anything wrong?" That young voice of hers quavered in fear. "Am I in trouble?"

"You did willingly get yourself caught in the middle of something messy."

"I just did what I was told to do," she said defensively.

"True enough. You were an obedient employee. It's not your fault that your employer is a murderer."

Phoebe let out a gasp. Several people did. Pippa merely sat there in blank-faced silence.

"Junior dumped you, didn't he, Pippa? He'd found genuine happiness with Mona and wanted nothing more to do with you. And I'm guessing he got awfully damned fed up with the way you kept peppering him with phone messages, too. In order to get rid of you, he must have really pissed you off. What was it he said to you when he finally decided to call you back?"

"Awful, hateful things," she recalled angrily, her eyes blazing. "He called me a bossy old hag. He told me my vagina was so dried out it was crusty and that my nipples were as inviting as a pair of raisins from the Mesozoic Era. He said he was sorry he'd ever gotten involved with me and told me to leave him the hell alone." Pippa broke off before she added, "People don't talk to me that way!"

"And then," I went on, "you had Tiffany tail me to Mona's apartment and report back to you so you could make use of that second steak knife you'd taken to pierce the eyeball of whomever it turned out had committed the cardinal sin of stealing him away from you."

Pippa curled her lip in distaste. "Her apartment was filth. She was filth."

"Actually, she was a major radical artist whose contribution to rock music will be remembered long after you and your snooty magazine are gone. She also made Junior happy. You didn't. You don't make any man happy. Your husband couldn't get far enough away from you."

"You killed him?!" Phoebe was starting to breathe heavily in and out, which Lulu took keen notice of, crouching there between her and Merilee. "You murdered my husband?" She let out a screech of outrage and then, with shocking speed and savagery, sweet, gentle Phoebe yanked a third Claude Dozorme rosewood-handle steak knife from the sleeve of her sweater, brandished it over her head, and dove across the coffee table, clearly intending to plunge it into her terrified mother's eyeball.

She never got there. Lulu was too fast for her—leaped across the table a split second before Phoebe did and clamped her jaws around her wrist, forcing Phoebe to drop the knife. Both the knife and Phoebe fell to the glass-covered steamer trunks. I quickly shoved the knife in Golden's direction as Phoebe lay there clutching her wrist in pain.

"Lulu bit me," she moaned in protest. "I'm bleeding!"

"Here, let me have a look," I said. "No, you're not. She didn't even break the skin. Just bruised it. You're such a good girl, Lulu." She let out a low whoop as I patted her. "For this, you'll get two anchovies when we get home."

"But it hurts," Phoebe continued to protest.

"You ought to be thanking her instead of complaining," Merilee said. "She just saved you from making the biggest mistake of your life."

One of the patrolmen helped Phoebe to her feet. "Should I cuff her, Loo?" he asked Golden.

"I would," he said as he bagged and tagged the knife.

The patrolman did, mindful of Phoebe's bruised wrist. Then he stood there with her next to the fireplace, firmly gripping her by the arm. Phoebe seemed calm and collected now. Her usual self.

The same could not be said for Pippa, who still looked utterly terrified.

Golden shook his head at me. "I don't get it. When did she grab that knife?"

"She was over by the knife drawer when she was making the coffee."

"But why did she grab it?"

"Because she knew. I think she's known all along that Pippa was the killer, haven't you, Phoebe?"

Phoebe nodded her head slowly up and down. "Yes, because Mother is evil," she said as she started to squirm in the patrolman's grasp.

"Settle down," I said to her. "Don't make things any worse for yourself. It's over now. We know what happened, and Pippa will pay a steep price for what she did."

"Just try to and build a case against me," Pippa dared Golden. Now that her fear had passed, her normal overbearing nature seemed fully restored. "If you take what you have to Bob Morgenthau, he'll throw it out." Robert Morgenthau was the Manhattan district attorney.

"Don't think so," Golden said quietly. "You were scrupulously tidy here when you stabbed Junior, but you left trace evidence behind at Mona's. There are fingerprints on her doorknob and towel rack that I have zero doubt will match yours. Sloppy. You got sloppy."

"I was in a hurry to get out of that rodent-infested hellhole."

"Just out of curiosity, are you HIV positive?" I asked her.

"Absolutely not. I insisted Junior wear a condom. I counsel all of my readers to insist on it."

"Lieutenant, am I in trouble?" Tiffany asked fretfully.

"That's not up to me to decide. The DA could make a case that you were an accessory before the fact to Mona's murder by following Hoagy to her place. I don't know if there'll be much desire to pursue that, since it appears you were simply doing what your employer told you to do, same as she told you to make those fake phone calls to the Sherry-Netherland . . ." Golden thumbed his chin. "But you do have a history of behaving badly, Tiffany. Got yourself kicked out of Yale for plagiarism. You might want to think about cleaning up your act."

"I can do something about that," Siena spoke up.

Tiffany peered at her. "You can? What?"

"I'll help you get a real estate license. I can coach you on taking the exam and find you a spot with an agency. You'll make a terrific Realtor. You're beautiful, stylish, well spoken, have an Ivy League pedigree, and are slippery, as Hoagy so aptly put it. You'll be a natural."

Tiffany shook her head. "I don't get it. Why do you want to help me?"

"Because you need a future, and I need someone to mentor. It'll take my mind off my troubles."

"Oh . . ." Tiffany thought it over. "Okay, thanks."

"You might want to do that now, Mrs. Longworth," Golden said to Pippa.

"Do what?" she demanded.

"Call your lawyer. Have him meet you at the Nineteenth Precinct house. I haven't formally placed you under arrest for the murders of Junior Singleton and Mona Dale, or read you your rights, but I will as soon as I take you in. He'll want to be there." He glanced around the room. "Phoebe will also have to be brought in for questioning."

"Questioning?" Pippa roared. "What's to ask? She just tried to kill me!"

"Take them both in," Golden told a patrolman. "In separate cars."

"Right, Loo. Should I cuff Mrs. Longworth?"

"I would."

"This is outrageous!" Pippa protested, struggling in the patrolman's grasp.

"This'll go a lot easier if you don't fight me, ma'am."

"Do you have any idea who I am?" she demanded furiously.

The patrolman didn't bother to answer her.

"As to the rest of you, you're free to go," Golden said. "But please don't leave town. We'll need witness statements from each one of you. You may also be asked to testify should Mrs. Longworth's case come to trial."

Siena Bing, Tiffany Tatum, Jill Perlo, Barry Zallinger, and Jon Porterfield began to file somberly out of the house.

Jon paused to thank me.

"For what?"

"Clearing it up. I'm going to miss that wild bastard, you know that? Life was never dull when he was around." Then he left with the others.

The patrolmen led Pippa and Phoebe out after that. Phoebe had a glazed, remote look on her face. Didn't even seem to notice Merilee standing there.

Katie and Bridget went to work gathering up plates and cups and taking them into the kitchen.

"I'll take care of that," Merilee said to them. "You're not here to work."

"It's no bother," Katie said, glancing at Merilee hesitantly. "I never liked Junior, you know. I thought he was a mean bastard who treated Phoebe like dirt. And I hate that my Bridget is carrying his baby. But we'll make out okay."

"Of course you will," Merilee said. "That reminds me—I promised you an autograph, Bridget." She grabbed a sheet of notepaper by the phone, scrawled a brief message, signed it, and handed it to her.

"Wow, thanks!" Bridget said after she'd read it.

"What'd she say?" Katie asked her.

"That she hoped we'd always be friends."

"Very nice of you," Katie said approvingly. "What's going to happen to Phoebe, do you think?"

"That's a good question," Merilee said. "Lieutenant, what's going to happen to Phoebe?"

"For starters, they'll probably park her in the psych ward at Bellevue overnight and make an evaluation in the morning. I'm assuming she has no prior history of violent behavior."

"That's correct," Merilee said.

"Just the world's worst mother," I said.

He grimaced. "I don't disagree. She may have to serve some mandatory criminal psych ward time. Then again, they may decide to cut her a little slack, considering the hell that she's been put through this week."

"Lieutenant, may we leave town?" Merilee asked.

"Why, where are you going?"

"On our honeymoon, which got slightly delayed."

He softened. "Oh, right. Sure thing. Merilee, it was a genuine thrill to meet you." Then he shook my hand and said, "Hoagy, I had my doubts, but

Lieutenant Mitry wasn't wrong about you." On hearing the small yip at his feet, he added, "Or about your sidekick."

"It was a pleasure to partner up with you, Lieutenant," I said. "Actually, I lied. It was a nightmare, but we got to the bottom of it, and that's all that matters. Oh, hey, before I forget . . ." I removed a business card from my wallet and handed it to him. "Gerald at Paul Stuart is expecting your call."

He frowned at it. "That's the fancy men's clothing store on Madison Avenue, isn't it?"

"Not fancy. Just top quality. I've given him a detailed list of your wardrobe needs."

"Needs? What needs?"

"The basics. Two suits, a navy blue and a gray flannel, a tweed blazer, slacks, cotton shirts, silk ties, cashmere socks, two pairs of rubber-soled brogans, one black, one cordovan, and a new topcoat."

He gaped at me, flabbergasted. "That'll cost thousands."

"Not to worry. I have a charge account there."

"I'll never be able to pay you back. I don't make that kind of money."

"But I do. When I was writing my novel, I lived hand-to-mouth for four years. Now that I've struck it rich, I can afford to do things for special people. You're a special person and you're going places, but you need to look the part. Just promise me you'll throw out every article of clothing you currently own."

"I-I don't know what to say."

"It's simple. Say yes."

"I can't. You've got to let me repay you somehow."

"Not necessary."

"Actually, I have a thought," Merilee said with an impish grin on her face. "I've always wanted to learn how to pole dance. Do you think Abby would be willing to teach me?"

"She decided to retire when things started getting serious between us."

"But she hasn't forgotten how, has she?"

"Oh, heck no. She still knows all the moves, believe me."

"In which case she'd be helping me to make a certain tall guy very happy for years to come, if you read me."

He grinned at her. "I read you. Merilee, you just made yourself a deal."

AUTHOR'S NOTE

Those of you who were around in 1983, and on top of the news, may note that I took a small historical liberty here. As a former journalist, I always try to be as accurate as possible, but sometimes fact and fiction get into a head-on collision and I'm forced to remind myself that I'm a storyteller now, and what you've just read is a work of fiction.